the
SECRETS
we
KEEP

the
SECRETS
we
KEEP

TRISHA LEAVER

Farrar Straus Giroux · New York

Farrar Straus Giroux Books for Young Readers
175 Fifth Avenue, New York 10010

Copyright © 2015 by Trisha Leaver
All rights reserved
Printed in the United States of America
Designed by Elizabeth H. Clark
First edition, 2015
1   3   5   7   9   10   8   6   4   2

macteenbooks.com

Library of Congress Cataloging-in-Publication Data
Leaver, Trisha.
    The secrets we keep / Trisha Leaver.
        pages cm
    Summary: "When her identical twin sister, Maddy, is
killed in a car accident, seventeen-year-old Ella assumes
Maddy's life, only to discover that it was filled with dark
secrets"—Provided by publisher.
    ISBN 978-0-374-30046-3 (hardback)
    ISBN 978-0-374-30048-7 (e-book)
    [1. Sisters—Fiction.   2. Twins—Fiction.   3. Death—
Fiction.   4. Identity—Fiction.   5. Conduct of life—Fiction.
6. High schools—Fiction.   7. Schools—Fiction.]   I. Title.

PZ7.L428Sec 2015
[Fic]—dc23
                                                        2014023372

Farrar Straus Giroux Books for Young Readers may be purchased
for business or promotional use. For information on bulk purchases
please contact Macmillan Corporate and Premium Sales
Department at (800) 221-7945 x5442 or by
email at specialmarkets@macmillan.com.

For my blackbird

the

SECRETS

we

KEEP

PROLOGUE

I don't remember her room being so cold. Even snuggled into her sweater the chill seeps in, settling into my bones like a whisper from beyond. That's where I will sleep tonight . . . in Maddy's bed, surrounded by her scent. Mom wants to change the sheets, but I won't let her. The hints of vanilla and lavender mingled with Alex's dark cologne brings a little piece of my sister back to me each night.

The only thing I have left of my old life is a few sketches and a poor replica of the friendship bracelet Josh gave me. It took me days to re-create, to weave the strings into the right pattern. It's not perfect, but it goes with me everywhere, a pathetic reminder of who I once was and what Josh still means to me. The real bracelet is gone, cut off and tossed aside just like my life.

I want to make peace with my choice, but Maddy's

secret haunts me. The dark pieces of her life are hidden in the back of her closet for no one but me to see. She's not who I thought she was, but that doesn't matter. Maddy was my sister, my twin sister, and I'll do anything for her, including losing myself.

1

My phone vibrated on my nightstand, jarring me from the sketchbook I had open on my lap. I'd re-created the same drawing five times in the past week, and yet it still wasn't good enough. Problem was, if I didn't figure it out by midnight tomorrow, I'd be out of time.

Assuming it was Josh again, I let it go to voice mail, more concerned with perfecting the sketch than bickering with him over something his neighbor and sometime-girlfriend, Kim, had said. I wasn't interested in dissecting why she was offended that Josh chose to let me drive him to school every day, even though she lived less than a hundred yards from him and he had a car of his own. That was his problem, not mine. And if he couldn't figure that one out on his own, then he was an idiot.

I tossed my charcoal pencil down in favor of graphite. Perhaps it was the reflection of light in my picture that was off. After a few strokes, I realized it wasn't—all I'd done was take a relatively decent drawing and make it worse.

The phone rang again, the same irritating song breaking my concentration. Swearing, I caught it before it buzzed off my nightstand and tossed it onto the bed next to me. Josh knew I was finishing up my portfolio tonight. I wanted it in early to ensure I was on track for early admission and not slotted into the general-admission pool for the Rhode Island School of Design. His call could wait; he'd understand.

The phone kept ringing, only stopping long enough to chime with an incoming text. Shaking my head, I turned to check the time. The bright numbers on my alarm clock bothered my bleary eyes. After several long, hard blinks and a few more muttered curses, the numbers came into focus. Two twenty-three in the effin morning. What could be so important that Josh had to call me at two-thirty in the morning?

I rubbed my eyes and answered, not bothering to check the caller ID. "What do you want now, Josh?"

"Ella? It's me."

It took a second for me to place the voice. It sounded off, throaty, and quieter than usual. I stared at the phone. My mind registered that it was my sister talking, but I still searched my darkened room for her. I don't know why; we hadn't shared a room since we were ten.

She was in bed when I came upstairs earlier that night. She was grounded. Dad had come home early from work on Tuesday and caught her and Alex in her bedroom. She worked him down from three weeks without a phone to one night of grounding, but that left her stuck at home on a Saturday night with nothing but me and her collection of DVDs to keep her company. So what was she doing on the other end of my phone?

Flicking on the hallway light, I stared across the narrow space to her room. As always, her door was closed, and I had to get up, trudge those seven steps to her door, and push it open. The room was quiet, her rumpled bed empty. The window behind it was open a crack, probably so she could sneak back in.

"Maddy? Where are you?"

"Alex's," she said, her voice muffled by what I could've sworn were tears.

"What's the matter?"

I was more curious than anything. Maddy didn't cry. Ever. She said it was a sign of weakness and that it made your makeup run. The weakness part I got; the popular crowd she'd immersed herself in would use anything they could against one another.

The makeup part . . . yeah, that I didn't get.

"Nothing. It doesn't matter. I just need a ride home, Ella."

"Where's your car?"

My guess was that she'd lost her keys or, better yet, was too drunk at one of Alex's parties to drive. I'd pick her up—there was no question about that, but I wanted to prod her for a reason first.

7

"It's at home. Jenna picked me up."

"It's two-thirty in the morning, Maddy," I said, already putting on my shoes. "Can't you get Jenna or Alex or somebody else to drive you home?"

"No, Alex can't and Jenna won't."

I shrugged, not caring that Maddy couldn't see me. I didn't get why Maddy hung out with Jenna, what she could possibly see in her best friend.

"Come on, Ella. If Mom and Dad find out I snuck out, I'm screwed."

I snorted at that one. Screwed? My twin sister was never screwed. She always seemed to skate by, knew exactly what to say to get herself out of everything. She'd be extra-sweet to our mother, pout for our father, and for Alex . . . well, from what I could gather, she had an entirely different arsenal for getting her way with him.

I could count my friends on one finger, but she could fill the entire cafeteria with laughter. I'd wake up at six in the morning so I could be early for school, and she'd roll in five minutes past the first bell, moaning about some flat tire to get herself out of detention. I'd collapse on my bed exhausted from studying till midnight, and she'd sneak out and go to a party with her boyfriend.

"I'm sure you'll think of something to tell them." And they'd buy it. No matter who she was talking to or what lie she was selling, they always bought it.

Maddy managed to make the honor roll, but that was mostly my doing. I'd study for days, then cave when she'd beg me to *pretend* I was her and take a test she'd completely forgotten about. I never complained; it's not like she took any advanced courses, so it required no effort on my part.

I was getting so good at playing her that her friends couldn't tell us apart. I kept my hair long and stopped adding pink streaks to the underside to look more like her. I'd mastered her voice as well, knew exactly how to raise and lower the pitch to match her sarcasm.

She paid me fifty bucks to take an oral Spanish exam for her last week, one she "completely forgot I had." I scored her a solid 82. No point in getting her an A. She took my spot in Physics that day, pretending to be me so I wouldn't get a detention for skipping class. We had a pop quiz. She took it for me, scoring me a miserable 47. Now I was looking at doing extra-credit work for the rest of the term to even manage a B.

I got back at her though. Still pretending to be Maddy, I went and found Jenna and told her I wasn't feeling well and was staying home that night. Then I called Mom to tell her the same thing. Maddy was beyond pissed; she'd unintentionally got herself a Friday night at home in bed with Mom hovering and me gloating. As for Jenna . . . I'd never heard that girl scream so loud in my life, something about a family dinner to celebrate her birthday that Maddy had promised she'd be at. Oh well, not my problem.

"Ella, please," Maddy begged, pulling me from that memory. "I'll make it up to you. I swear. Whatever you want."

"You always say that, Maddy."

"I know, but I mean it this time. Please."

I had a memory full of promises just like that one. Difference was, I kept my promises. Maddy's were nothing more than hollow assurances aimed at getting people to do what she wanted.

We were so different. Maddy was skirts and heels and flatirons, where I was jeans and T-shirts and ponytails. She was Friday-night parties and homecoming dances. I was B-rated horror movies on the couch with microwave popcorn. From her perfect hair to her perfect friends, right down to her perfectly pedicured toes, Maddy was my opposite.

"Ella? Ella!" Maddy shouted into the phone.

The muffled crying I'd heard earlier was gone, her rapid breathing and rising pitch lending an edge of panic to her voice. I don't know why she'd freak; it's not like I'd ever say no. She was my sister, my twin sister at that, and I would always help her.

"Fine. Whatever," I said, and grabbed a sweatshirt from the end of my bed. "I'll be there in fifteen."

I quickly flipped through my drawings, picked the best of four sketches of the exact same subject, and carefully tore it out. Surprisingly, it was the first one I'd done. I scanned it in, adding it to the ones I'd already uploaded, and hit the Submit button. It was only October 18. The application wasn't due for another two weeks, but, like I said, I wanted it in early. Plus, if Maddy expected me to drop everything to come get her, then the least she could do was wait the ten extra minutes it'd take me to e-mail my art school application.

My dog, Bailey, hopped down off my bed the minute I stood up, intent on following me around. He beat me to my bedroom door, then waited as if he needed my permission. Knowing him, he'd bark the second I left the house, letting me know he was not happy staying behind. I didn't mind him being angry. He was a dog, he'd get over it in less than a second. What I didn't want was Bailey to wake my parents up. It was bad enough I had to go bail Maddy out. I didn't feel like dealing with Mom and Dad's questions, too.

I grabbed a treat from the box I kept on my nightstand and hid it beneath the covers on my bed. Bailey did as I expected; he jumped up and started nosing through my comforter. I'd hidden it deep enough that it would take Bailey a while to find, hopefully long enough for me to get out of the house unnoticed.

I poked my head into my parents' room before heading downstairs. They were asleep, the TV still casting a pale blue light. I thought about turning it off but figured the sudden lack of noise might wake them up. My eye caught the array of pictures covering Mom's dresser. The flickering glow from the TV gave a hint of what they were, but I didn't need to see the photos to describe each one. They'd been there for as long as I could remember.

The big one in the middle was a family portrait taken

three Christmases ago. We were gathered around a fake fireplace in some photographer's studio. The scowl on my face was the source of a huge argument that day. Next to that was a picture of Maddy and me on our sixteenth birthday. She looked stunning and was staring off into the distance, probably at Alex. I was standing there praying for Mom to hurry up and take the damn thing so I could go back to my room. The other three pictures were of Maddy. Maddy after her field hockey team won divisionals her sophomore year. Maddy and Alex at junior prom last year. Maddy with the keys to her "new" car.

It was the same in real life. At my father's office Christmas party, she was the one he introduced first. When we went to church, she got to sit between them. When a relative or an old friend asked my mom about the twins, it was Maddy's accomplishments Mom launched into first. Me they were still trying to figure out.

I was the smart, quiet one who preferred the inside of a book to parties. Quirky and reserved, that's how they described me to their friends. Quirky and reserved.

I quietly closed the door and made my way downstairs. It was pitch-black outside, the moon hidden behind a thick bank of clouds. It had rained earlier and, from the looks of it, was going to again.

I grabbed my coat and hat from the hall closet and headed outside. Luckily, the neighbors had left their porch lights on, or I would've walked smack into the trash cans at the end of our driveway. As it was, I'd already stumbled twice—once over Bailey's half-chewed rope toy and again, steps later, over a sprinkler head. That last one landed me on my butt, cursing and trying to brush the dampness from my jeans.

When I finally made it to my car, I realized Maddy's car was in the way. She'd parked straight across our driveway, blocking everybody in.

"Seriously, Maddy?" I said as I kicked her tire. It'd be fine if she was the first to leave in the morning, but she never was. Maddy was always the last one out the door, putting her makeup on in the rearview mirror while she raced to school. It was me who rearranged the cars each morning so Dad could get to work and I could get to school.

I winced at my throbbing toe and made my way back to the house. Moving the cars around wasn't an option. If turning off the TV had the potential to wake my parents up, then shuffling cars in the driveway would certainly have them stumbling down the stairs wondering where I was going.

I hung my keys on the hook next to the door. There were five hooks there, each clearly labeled with a name. Mine, Dad's, Mom's, Maddy's, even one designated for the lawn tractor keys, but Maddy's weren't there. Of course they wouldn't be there. Knowing her, she'd probably thrown them on the counter when she came in, figuring one of us would find them and hang them up.

"This is the last time, Maddy. I swear to God, this is the

last time I do anything for you," I muttered to myself as I fished around our kitchen counters in the dark. She couldn't make bailing her out easy. Nope, Maddy had to make everything as difficult as possible.

I finally found her keys wedged behind the radio. I picked them up, swearing to tear her a new one for being so selfish, then headed back out into the damp night air. If everything went as it should, I'd be home and in bed in less than a half hour with another of Maddy's promises to make it up to me stashed away in my brain.

2

It was drizzling by the time I reached Alex's house. Except for a few scattered cars parked between the trees, you'd never have known there was a party going on. I guess that was a perk of being *really* rich—a long drive-way and lots of land to buffer sound.

I remembered the day Maddy met Alex Furey. We were freshmen, and it was our third day of school. I thought going to a new school with my sister would make every-thing easier, figured I'd have at least one person to sit with at the lunch table. I didn't take into account that we had no classes together, that Maddy was a lot more outgoing than me, or that we had very little in common. I assumed we'd stick together, and I'd have a built-in safety net.

Maddy let me crowd her those first few days, smiling and encouraging me to go off on my own and make some new friends. I tried: sitting next to people who I didn't recognize in my classes and saying hi to the few kids who looked my way. But when none of them said hi back, I ignored them and minded my own business.

That first Wednesday, I went to find Maddy in the cafeteria, excited about the drawing I'd done in open studio. The lunchroom was as loud as always, the smell a cross between burned pizza and nasty gym socks. Looking forward to a half hour of peace, I grabbed a tray and bought something I deemed safe enough to eat—a hot dog—and headed in to find her. But she wasn't sitting in the corner of the cafeteria like she had been on Monday and Tuesday. That table was empty—eight vacant chairs surrounding an equally deserted table. I searched the other tables, automatically focusing on those kids sitting alone. No Maddy. It wasn't until I scanned the center of the room, my eyes skating across the six tables that had been jammed together, that I saw her. She wasn't sitting in a chair. She was perched on top of the table, her arms draped around some kid's neck. And she was laughing.

I stood there watching her, debating whether to go over and sit down next to her or to seek out one of the empty tables that littered the corners. Luckily, I didn't have to make the decision. Maddy made it for me.

She extricated herself from the boy's hold and hopped down off the table. I couldn't hear her over the noise, but I gathered from the flick of her wrists that she was telling him she'd be back in a minute.

"Hey," she said as she stopped in front of me. "I waited for you outside the cafeteria, but—"

"Yeah, sorry, I had a question about a geometry problem," I said, cutting off her lie. She'd never waited for me outside before. Not once during junior high and not once since we started here.

"Who are they?" I asked, looking past her to the group of people now staring at us.

"Alex Furey," she said, smiling in his direction. Here was a smile I hadn't seen before—head cocked and perky.

"Okay," I said, taking a step toward the table. I didn't care who we sat with so long as I didn't have to sit alone.

Maddy stopped me, her perfectly pink nails encircling my wrist. I stared down at them, wondering when she'd had time to paint her nails and when she'd started wearing pink. And were those tiny white flowers painted in the middle?

We'd come to school looking nearly identical, so much so that our homeroom teacher did a double take. We were wearing the same jeans, the same hair twisted into a bun, the same boring beige tank tops when we left the house, but somehow she had changed and redone everything from her shoes to her makeup in the last three hours.

"Alex has a cousin your age. He thinks—"

"You mean *our* age," I interrupted.

She shrugged that off and steered me toward a table in the back of the cafeteria. "I think you'll like him. From what Alex says, you two have a lot in common."

Which translated to: he was smart, quiet, and too quirky for his own family to acknowledge. Apparently, so was I.

"He's starting an anime club," she continued, fingering the notebook I had tucked under my tray. It was covered with manga drawings I'd been working on during History class. Some of them were good; most of them were doodles. I had the one I wanted to show her on top. I'd ripped it out of my notebook, thinking I'd give it to her at lunch.

Maddy took the tray from my hands, not once looking at the drawing underneath. "Come on. I'll introduce you."

She was a good five steps ahead of me before my feet started moving. I tucked the drawing into my notebook and followed her over. The two kids sitting there looked up when she dropped my tray onto the table. I recognized both of them from Honors English but had no clue who they actually were. They were two guys with longish hair and Mountain Dew T-shirts eating their food and minding their own business until my sister interrupted them.

I swung my head from them to Maddy. Her food, if she had any, her books, and her phone were at the other table.

"It's Ella, right?" I turned toward one of the boys at the table and nodded, wondering how he knew my name. "I'm Josh."

"Yup, her name's Ella," Maddy offered up when I remained silent. "She's into that Japanese-cartoon stuff you guys like."

Maddy nudged me closer, and I stumbled into the corner of the table. "Right, Ella?"

I nodded, still confused, still mute. Until five minutes ago, she was into my "Japanese-cartoon stuff," too. Last I checked, she had an entire bulletin board dedicated to my drawings. Now she was talking about it like it was some noxious side effect of having an identical twin sister. I followed her gaze to the other table and watched as her entire personality changed instantly in front of my eyes. She shook her head, tossing her hair as she smothered a giggle. Alex winked, and I swore she blushed.

"You're good, right?" Maddy asked over her shoulder as she danced away. I didn't bother to answer. I was too busy trying to figure out what the hell was going on.

"You gonna sit?" Josh asked.

"What?"

"I said are you going to sit?"

"Yeah. I guess so."

I pulled out a chair a safe three seats away from him and sat down. I didn't speak, just focused on my food, confused and hurt that I'd been dumped—literally dumped—by my own sister.

Three years later I was still sitting at that same table with Josh, but now my sister's exclusion didn't bother me.

3

I parked as close to Alex's house as I could, which was still fifteen cars away. I could hear the music now, the faint thump of the bass echoing through the windows. Out of habit, I locked the car. Not that anybody would think to steal it. My sister's ten-year-old Honda was nothing special compared to the shiny new toys parked around it. That, and nobody messed with anything that belonged to Alex Furey. And my sister most definitely belonged to him.

I followed the music up the walkway. The front porch was littered with plastic cups and empty pizza boxes, the occasional soda can tossed in between. I made my way up the stairs, careful not to look at the two kids making out on the railing, and opened the door to the house.

I don't know what hit me first, the music or the smell, but both sent me in search of clean air. Three steps and the stench of perfume, pot, and sweat finally cleared. The pounding in my head . . . well, that dulled to a tolerable level. I hadn't been to a party like this since I was a freshman and Mom paid Maddy to take me out with her. Something about me needing to make friends. Since then, I'd spent plenty of time running pick-up duty but had done my best to avoid *ever* having to enter into this social scene again.

"Hey, what are you doing here?"

His voice echoed over the drumming in my head, and I looked up to see Josh coming out the front door. I thought about asking him the same question—he wasn't exactly top man on his cousin's list—then I remembered his parents were away, Alex's with them. A family vacation that didn't include kids.

Surprisingly, both sets of parents thought it wiser if Josh and Alex stayed together while they were gone. My guess was that that had nothing to do with Josh's parents and everything to do with Alex's father wanting to make sure his son didn't trash his house while they were gone. Josh would stay to make his parents happy, but there was no way he'd run babysitting duty for his uncle.

"Looking for Maddy," I said. "She called and said she needed a ride home."

"Stay for a while and hang out with me. I brought some movies from home. We can watch them upstairs."

He'd been bugging me for weeks to spend more time with him, but I'd been obsessed with my art school application and passing AP Physics. Plus, he had Kim now, and she was more than willing to occupy every second of his time.

"Can't," I said. "I'm beat and we have a Physics test on Monday. Kinda hoping for something better than a B on this one." More accurately I needed an A to make up for the F Maddy scored me last week.

Josh shrugged, the slight bit of hope I'd seen in his eyes fading away. "Sent my application in this morning. You finish yours?"

"Yup. I submitted it before I left. Now we wait."

Josh laughed. We had planned this since the middle of freshman year. We'd submit our applications on the same day, to the same schools, then start obsessing about it four weeks out. When the e-mails finally came, we'd meet up and compare them. We'd go together or not at all. If one of us didn't get in, then, as far as we were concerned, neither of us did.

"Yeah, now we wait." He held the door open for me, and we walked in. It took a minute, but once I got used to the smell, it wasn't so bad. The house wasn't overly crowded, but that didn't make it any easier to get around. Nobody got out of our way, and we had to weave around people, furniture, and the occasional nasty glare to make our way through the living room.

"No Kim?" I asked, smirking. She'd been clingy lately, complaining that he spent too much time with me and not enough with her. I didn't see the problem; neither did Josh, but then again I wasn't the one dating a sophomore.

"Nope, seniors only, according to Alex," he said, and I gathered from his tone that Kim's absence wasn't bothering him. He'd spent the entire day with her while I was holed up in my room finishing the sketches for my RISD application. Knowing him, he was probably looking forward to some time without her.

I made my way through the house, irked when I saw some kid point in my direction and scowl. I could look and act exactly like my sister if I wanted to, had done it for years. But here, when I was being myself, I was a nothing.

"She was in the kitchen last time I saw her," Josh said as he pointed to the far side of the house. "But that was a while ago."

"What about you?"

"What about me?"

"Why didn't you offer to bring her home?"

"She never asked," he said, and I heard the inference in his voice. He would gladly have given Maddy a ride home . . . had she asked.

I couldn't help but look around as we made our way through the house. My sister had been dating Alex since freshman year, and I'd never once set foot in here. I'd picked her up at the end of the driveway plenty of times, had made it as far as the front door to ring the bell. But not once, before tonight, had I been invited in.

I scanned the room, wondering what made this kid so special. If it was there, I didn't see it. His house may have been bigger than ours, but the furniture looked no more expensive. The iPod docking station on the table looked to be a few years old. Mine was better.

I spotted the shadow of a girl curled up on the couch. She looked vaguely familiar, like someone I would've recognized instantly had the lights in the room not been so dim.

She sniffled and ran her sleeve across her nose. I followed her gaze to the far wall, wondering what had her so entranced. The wall was blank except for the giant flat screen mounted halfway up, and that was off.

"She okay?" I asked Josh.

"Who? Molly?" he asked. "I guess so. I talked to her earlier, asked her if she wanted a ride home or something. She said she was fine and wanted to be left alone."

I thought about confirming that for myself. As soon as I found Maddy, I was leaving anyway. I could drop her off. I made a mental note to check and see if she was still there before I left, then headed into the next room.

The kitchen was at the far end of the house and doubled as beer central. There was a keg on the floor, tucked into a brown trash barrel that I presumed was filled with ice. Two coolers stood by the sliding door and what was left of several pizzas littered the counter. There were people everywhere—jammed into the small corner between the refrigerator and the pantry, sitting on the counters, leaning against walls. They'd dragged the dining room chairs in so that they could fit twelve people around the table that housed a bunch of plastic cups and what looked like a Ping-Pong ball.

I scanned the room twice looking for Maddy, listening for the sound of her voice. Placing my hands on Josh's shoulders, I hoisted myself up so I could see, and still no sign of my sister.

"She's not here," I said as I glanced at my watch. So much for my back-in-bed-in-less-than-a-half-hour plan.

Josh looked around the room himself before moving toward a kid by the door. "You seen Maddy Lawton around?"

The kid looked at us, then opened the cooler. He dug around in the slush before pulling out a hard lemonade. His eyes met mine and he smirked, no doubt too drunk to figure out that I was not my sister. I remembered him from Maddy's Spanish class. Keith something or other. He sat next to her and had asked if "she" wouldn't mind sharing the answers to the oral exam *I'd* taken. I batted my eyes, and in my best Maddy voice said, "Absolutely, darling. Anything for you," then wrote the wrong answers down and slid them toward the edge of my desk. He winked and quickly memorized them, never once questioning who I was. Idiot.

Josh caught Keith's look and clarified. "This is Ella," he said. "We're trying to find Maddy."

"Ha! Well, that explains why she looks like crap," Keith said as he walked away, not offering to help.

I glanced down at myself, thought maybe I was wearing mismatched shoes or had a big pizza stain on my sweatshirt. I had on an old pair of jeans, a plain gray hoodie, and an equally dull jacket, and nothing was grossly wrong with any of them. Sneakers matched, too, so maybe it was my hair. I'd quickly tossed it into a ponytail before I left, then tucked it up under my hat. Perhaps I should have actually brushed it.

Josh caught my hand as I went to smooth my hair. "You look fine. He's just being a jerk."

Not wanting Josh to know how much the drunk kid's comments hurt, I tried for a smile. I doubted I had pulled it off.

"I wasn't lying, you look fine," Josh said again. "You always do."

I shook my head and watched as Keith stopped a few feet away and bent down to whisper something into a girl's ear. She turned around, her gaze raking over me. Crap, Jenna.

She walked over, a beer in one hand and the drunk kid's hand locked in the other. The disgusted scowl she reserved for me was firmly in place. "What are you doing here?" Jenna asked. "I strongly doubt *you* are on the guest list."

"Where's Maddy?" I asked, ignoring her comment.

"She's gonna flip when she finds out you're here. God, it is bad enough she has to deal with you at school, but here . . ." She shook her head and trailed off, unable to find the exact words to describe her hatred of me.

26

"Whatever. Where's Maddy?"

I followed Jenna's eyes to the ceiling and groaned. It would be exactly like my sister to call me in a tizzy, then suck down two more beers and forget about everything. "You've got to be kidding me."

Jenna giggled, her hand playing with the blond hair at the back of the drunk kid's neck. She was amazing, could go from mean girl to flirt at a staggeringly impressive speed. Yeah . . . me, I didn't find it amusing.

"You want to check upstairs?" Josh asked, motioning toward the stairs.

"Uh . . . no," I said, remembering the one time I walked into Maddy's room unannounced to retrieve the calculator she'd "borrowed" from me. Mom was out at book club and Dad still wasn't home from work, otherwise I doubt Alex would've even set foot in Maddy's room. Dad made sure both Alex and Maddy knew the rule—no boys upstairs if my parents weren't home and even when they were, the door had to stay open. Wide open. That night the door was closed, and I got more of a view of Alex than I ever wanted.

"Let's look outside. If she's not there, I'll check upstairs," Josh said.

I nodded my thanks and followed Josh onto the deck. What the house lacked on the inside, it made up for out here. It was quiet, the huge lawn sloping down toward the lake. I could see a shape I thought was a dock, but without a light, I couldn't be sure.

But what I could see clearly were two Adirondack chairs off to the side of the deck stairs. And if my eyes were right, someone was sitting in one of them.

"Maddy?" I said as I approached. She was huddled into herself, curled up in a ball, her shoes dangling from her hands.

"Maddy?" I repeated, shaking her gently. I'd never seen her like this—quiet and distant—and it was beginning to freak me out. "What's wrong?"

She looked up, and the fear that had struck me when I first saw her had nothing on the pain that lanced my heart now. The tears I'd heard on the phone were still there, streaming down her face as she struggled to compose herself. From the looks of it, she'd been sobbing long and hard, hidden away back here.

I shot Josh a glance, hoping he could fill me in. He'd been here the whole time, was sleeping under the same roof as Alex. He had to have some idea as to what was going on.

Josh shrugged, hunched down in front of my sister, and stared into her eyes. He waited a second for Maddy to silently acknowledge him before asking, "Where's Alex?"

"Inside." She hiccuped.

"Do you want me to get him?"

"No," she said, and stood up.

She was soaking wet and shaking, her lips nearly blue. From the dampness of the grass and the puddle next to the deck, I gathered it had rained here, too. And by the looks of it, Maddy had been sitting outside, alone, when it happened.

I doubted she was drunk. She got up without any help and didn't seem to have a problem following my questions. She didn't stumble or cover her mouth and swallow down beer-tinged bile threatening to come up. I knew what drunk Maddy looked like, and this wasn't it.

My guess was that the glaze covering her eyes was from her tears and nothing more. "What's going on?" I asked.

She stared at me for a long minute, then shook her head. "Nothing. Can we go?"

I had a thousand questions for her, but I knew she wouldn't answer any of them. I thought about searching each room of the house until I found Alex and asking *him* what was going on. Somehow I didn't think that would help. If Maddy didn't want me to know, then she wouldn't tell me. I'd hear about it on Monday at school, then get a completely different version of the story the following day. By the end of the week, I'd have fifteen versions of "What Happened to Maddy Lawton?" to sift through. But before I listened to any of them, I wanted the real story from her.

I let it slide for now, more interested in getting her shivering body into the warm car than anything else. Tomorrow . . . tomorrow I'd start asking the questions.

4

I didn't bother to take us through the house. I figured my sister was out here by herself for a reason—a reason that probably involved her friends *not* seeing her like this.

"You want me to follow you home?" Josh asked.

I shook my head. His car was blocked in five deep, and if I didn't get home soon, my father, and not my silently miserable sister, would be my biggest problem.

"Call me when you get home," Josh said, and pointed toward the house. A few people had found their way out onto the front lawn and were busy setting off car alarms. "I'll be up for a while."

Yeah, he'd be up for the rest of the night working cleanup duty while Alex passed out on the couch.

I got in the driver's seat and looked over at my sister. She was slumped down into her seat, staring straight ahead.

Her hair was damp, stringy, and hanging limply around her shoulders, and what little makeup she had on was now smudged.

"Your mascara is messed up," I said as I handed her a tissue from my pocket. It was damp from the rain, but that didn't matter; it'd work better that way.

She tossed the tissue aside and opened up her glove compartment, pulling out a small package of baby wipes. In three swipes, she had her face clean, every trace of her made-up face gone. Like this, natural, with no pretenses and no image to maintain, she looked a lot more like me.

A shiver racked her body and she drew her knees up to her chest, resting her head on them. Her eyes caught mine and she smiled, the faint tilt of the lips the closest thing to a thank-you I would get. My eyes shifted to her feet. They were bare. She was holding her flats when I found her. She'd probably dropped them when she stood up. I toyed with going back to get them, grabbing a coat of Alex's for her while I was at it, but I didn't want to waste any more time.

I took off my coat and tugged my sweatshirt up over my head, then gave it to her along with my coat and hat. I was quite sure I was going to freeze my butt off until the heat kicked in. But she was pale and she was shivering. I didn't know what else to do.

Maddy took my sweatshirt and slid her arms into the sleeves, then put my coat on over it. She wrapped it farther around herself, sinking deeper into the fabric and herself in the process. She didn't complain about her hair when I tucked it into my hat, nor did I get a thank-you when I gave her my socks and shoes. She merely shoved her feet into them and went back to staring out the passenger-side window.

Not long ago, she would've said thank you, and probably wouldn't have taken the only dry clothes I had in the first place. But a lot can change in a few years. *She'd* changed a lot in a few years.

I cranked up the heat and searched the rest of her car for a blanket, an extra sweater, an old pair of jeans... anything I could find to still her tremors. I found a tube of lip gloss, an empty Pop-Tarts box, and three days' worth of homework that hadn't been turned in. Funny, it was Spanish homework. Now I knew why she had needed me to take that test.

"We'll be home in a few minutes," I said as I tried to maneuver the car off the lawn and onto the driveway. It was harder than I thought with bare feet—my toes kept slipping off the pedal. "I'll cover for you tomorrow with Mom and Dad and tell everybody at school on Monday that you aren't feeling well if you want to stay home for a couple of days and avoid everybody."

"Can't," she mumbled. "People will start talking if I don't show, make up some rumor about me and Alex fighting."

Judging by the stares of the few people we'd passed

in the front yard, my guess was they already were. "They started talking before you left, Maddy. Trust me."

"No they didn't. They wouldn't do that. Alex wouldn't let them."

I groaned, amazed at the lie she was selling herself. "You honestly believe that? The rumors started the second I got there, the instant they realized that you called *me* to come get you rather than ask Alex to drive you home."

I didn't bother to tell her about Jenna or her dig at me. Maddy would take her side. She always did, blamed Jenna's miserable attitude on the fact that she had a hard time at home. As if her parents' financial problems and their crazy need to hide them were somehow a free pass for Jenna to be mean. But no amount of lipstick could cover up her ugly personality.

She shrugged. "You don't get it, Ella. You never will. They don't care about you showing up. They don't care about you at all. They're more interested in lying—making up stories that will ruin their friends' lives while making themselves more popular."

She was absolutely right. Since we started high school, I'd watched her dance around these people, play their games, and worry about what everybody thought while I cleaned up her messes. I didn't get any of it. Not from the first time she sat down at Alex's lunch table to last month when she came home so trashed from a party at the beach that I had to spend three hours with her in the bathroom holding her hair back while she puked. Once she passed out, I had the honor of lying to my parents, telling them the leftover Chinese food Maddy had inhaled when she got home was probably bad. That wasn't the first time I'd covered for Maddy, and it sure wouldn't be the last.

The first hailstones hit the hood of the car like a steel drum hammering through my head. I turned the wipers on, but one was broken, a quarter of the rubber hanging off the blade. It did little to get rid of the water, rather smoothed it into a giant smear across the glass. Craning my head to see through the one clear spot, I pulled out onto the road.

The familiar chime of an incoming text had me glancing Maddy's way. She whipped her phone out and started typing, pausing only long enough to angle the heat vents toward herself.

"Damage control going well over there?"

"What?" she asked, not bothering to look up from her phone.

"I asked if you had everything figured out over there. If you and Jenna got your stories straight."

"What does Jenna have to do with anything?"

Jenna had everything to do with it. As far as I was concerned, she was the one who'd taken my sister away from me, introduced her to that crowd of popular people, and kept her there. If it wasn't for Jenna, I'd still have my sister . . . my best friend. The one who used to camp out with me every Fourth of July in the backyard. The one who always gave me the bottom part of her ice cream cone for my baby doll Sarah. The one who took away the book *Your Body and You* that Mom had given me in the sixth grade and gave me her own, unadulterated version of the truth. Jenna had taken *that* Maddy away from me without asking, and I wanted her back.

"Jenna has everything to do with it," I yelled. "Everything!"

Apparently I'd hit a nerve because for the first time since we got in the car she put her phone down and looked at me. "You have no idea what Jenna's life is like. None whatsoever."

Maybe not, but I didn't care either way. "Doesn't matter," I said as I turned my eyes back to the road. "No matter how you slice it, she is still a mean, selfish cow."

I didn't need to look at my sister to tell she was getting annoyed. I could feel it, the air around us so thick with tension it was suffocating. "What's your problem, Ella?"

I don't know if it was my irritation with the wipers, that I was now freezing without my coat or shoes while she sucked up the heat, or because I was simply exhausted, nervous about getting into RISD, and stressed about the Physics test I still had to study for, but I snapped.

"My problem? *My problem?* I don't know, how about the fact that I dropped everything to come and pick you up, yet you won't tell me why? But the people who wouldn't leave their beers long enough to drive you home . . . they get the whole story."

She glanced at me, her mouth opening once to speak

35

before she shut it and waved me off. "You wouldn't understand."

"You're right, I don't. You worry so much about what they will think and say, but I'm the one who's always bailing you out. I'm the one who took your Spanish test last week so that you could pass and not get kicked off the field hockey team for failing a class. I'm the one who's tired and freezing my butt off over here so Mom and Dad won't find out that you snuck out. The least you could do is—"

"You want your coat back, here, take it."

She took off the shoulder portion of her seat belt and tucked it under her arm, then tugged at the sleeves of my jacket. I held my hand up to stop her. I didn't want the coat; she could sleep in it for all I cared. "It's not about the coat, Maddy. It's about me always having to pick up your pieces."

"I never asked you to—"

"You called me. You. Called. Me. *Me!*"

"Maybe," she said, and shrugged. "But you didn't have to come."

I had to swallow hard to hold back my tears. I'd always done whatever she asked. But no matter what I did or how far I went for her, she'd kept me on the outside, five safe steps away from her and her inner circle.

When we were kids, I knew everything about her. We had one diary until the age of thirteen. One. Each day one of us would write in it, then hand it to the other to read and write her own entry. The embarrassment I felt on my first day of middle school when I tripped and fell in the cafeteria, my lunch going everywhere. The pain Maddy felt when she found out the boy she liked in seventh grade bet his friends he could get her to make out with him in the janitor's closet. And the fear and excitement that first time we went off to camp the summer before fifth grade, wondering if people would like us, but not really caring because we had each other. Back then we shared everything, including those things that were too embarrassing to say out loud. Now, I was lucky if I got a nod of acknowledgment as I passed her in the hall.

"I'm not doing this anymore, Maddy. You're on your own with school, with Mom and Dad, with everything."

"Wait . . . What? Why?" She anxiously rattled the questions off, not giving me time to answer before continuing. "You can't do that. If they find out, I'm screwed. They'll ground me for weeks. I can't. Alex's birthday is next week, and the Snow Ball is coming up, plus Jenna's having a— you can't. You're my sister, you can't."

"Not my problem."

"Why, Ella? Why are you doing this to me?"

"I'm not doing anything. That's the point, Maddy. I'm not doing anything for you anymore. Like I said, you're on your own. I do all the work and you get—"

"You're jealous. You're doing this because you're jealous."

I didn't bother to respond to that. It was a ridiculous thing for her to say and completely untrue. The last thing

I wanted was to be her, constantly worrying about what I looked like, who I was dating, and watching what I said. She was always on, always pretending to be perfect. Too much work for me.

"Do you know what I'd give to be like you?" she asked. "How much easier it is for that nameless person in the back of the class who doesn't have to worry about what people think or how they . . ."

I didn't hear what she said next, I was still trying to process the nameless-person-who-no-one-gave-a-damn-about comment. I mean, I wasn't an idiot. I knew what people thought of her versus what they thought of me. The countless pictures of her on my parents' bureau, the massive number of people who seemed to gravitate toward her at school, and the fifty thousand text messages she got each day compared to my ten were evidence enough. Hearing her say it though—my own sister admitting that nobody in school cared much about who I was—somehow made it real.

"That's who you think I am?" I asked, unable to hide the small quiver in my voice. "That's what you and everybody else think?"

"What do you care?" she fired back, obviously still angry. "According to you, who cares what people think?"

People . . . yeah. But she wasn't some random kid at school. She was my sister.

I wanted out of that car, away from her. Forget the rain, I'd walk home. It'd take me over three hours to walk those ten miles, but I didn't care. Let Maddy scramble to come up with an excuse as to why I wasn't there when Dad got up to walk Bailey and found my room empty. Knowing her, she'd shrug and claim she'd been asleep and had no clue where I was. But I'd fix that. As soon as I walked in that door, as soon as Dad let the first question fly, I'd fix that.

"Picking me up is the least you can do for me," she continued, her voice rising to a deafening pitch. "After everything I've done for you, the people I've—"

"You've never done anything for me!" I fired back. "Since the day you set foot in Cranston High, you haven't done anything for me. It's as if I'm not your sister anymore, as if you are too embarrassed to be seen with me."

"You have no idea what they say about you, Ella," she griped. "How many times I've had to make up excuses for the way you act and dress."

"Oh, I've heard it. Jenna made sure—"

"You think Jenna is the worst of it? You have no clue. You think *you* cover for *me*? You should hear the things *I* have to say to my friends to explain your lack of social skills. *Ella is shy. Ella is quiet. Ella gets nervous around people.*"

She stopped yelling at me long enough to catch her breath, to let her irritation morph into pure anger. "You sit there with your one friend and look at the rest of us like we're idiots. Well, you know what? You're the selfish one, and I'm sick of your crap! I'm sick of you always acting like you're better than me when we both know you're not!"

I slammed on the brakes and yanked the wheel hard to the right. The sooner I was away from her the better. She grabbed the armrest, the sudden jerk of the car taking her off guard. Good. About time. I wanted her off guard.

For a brief second, I felt the tires catch the road, the tremor in the wheel as I forced the car to turn when it didn't want to. The friction eased, and the wheel stopped shaking. The car slid in every direction. I felt a sharp tug on the wheel, and I wrenched it back, trying to make the car go straight. I pressed the brake to the floor, demanding that the car stop, but it kept floating along.

I saw the side of the road, the three-inch concrete curb that separated us from the trees. There was no ear-piercing shriek, no grabbing for the door to brace myself. Nothing but complete and utter silence.

The car teetered when it hit the curb but didn't stop. It spun sideways and continued on its path. I turned and saw the same horrified gaze on Maddy's face that I knew was on mine. Her eyes widened and her lips parted on a silent scream as the trees grew bigger, grew closer.

I heard, saw, and felt it in slow-motion. Branches scraped across the top of the roof, each grinding sound showering the windshield with dead leaves. The car shook, bounced to the left, skimming the trunk of a tree. I watched it happen, saw the bark peeling away, a pale blue streak of paint left in its place.

Maddy's cry shattered my own. Through the windshield, I could see the trees flying by. The car was still moving, picking up speed as it lurched to the right, balancing on the outer edges of its tires before tumbling over.

The thin tip of a branch snapped and fell on the hood of the car. I had a second of relief before I heard the windshield crack. My eyes fixed on the glass as I saw the crack spread, the circles widening and creeping out until the windshield finally shattered and coated me with shards of glass.

Somehow I had the presence of mind to brace myself, to grasp on to the steering wheel and lock my arms. I looked over at Maddy. She was screaming, her eyes closed and her hands flailing around for something to hold on to. Her hand brushed mine, and I grabbed it, clutching it with every ounce of strength I had.

There was no blinding light when we finally hit the tree, only burning pain followed by darkness. Total, desensitizing darkness.

5

Noise. That's what brought me out of the darkness
I was trapped in. Voices, alarms, the screech of metal, the
thud of running feet—all of it combined into one jumbled
mess of noise. I fought through the black fog, tried to grab
on to each faint sound, hoping it would pull me farther and
farther away from the massive weight that seemed to settle
upon me.

"No, not yet," someone yelled, and the hands I could
feel at my side vanished. I tried to move, to bring my fingers to my face and physically claw away the wet haze covering my eyes. But nothing would move. Not my arms, not
my head, not even my legs. It was as if my entire body was
crammed into a metal vise.

"Easy there." The voice was back, unfamiliar and soothing at the same time. I felt my eyelids being pried open, the
searing light burning into first my left eye, then the right.

They fell closed and the light disappeared, the pain lingering behind.

"Can you tell me your name?"

"We have to move." It was a woman now, her words sharp and curt.

Move? Move where? I wanted to sleep. Sleep? Wait. I couldn't sleep. I needed to go pick up Maddy. She'd called me from Alex's house, something about needing a ride home. Wait. No. I was at Alex's. She was crying out on the back lawn. That's why I was wet. Her tears were falling on me. Nope, that wasn't right. It was the rain.

I shook my head, tried to piece together the flashes of information. None of them made sense. She'd said I was the nameless girl. A nobody. That, I remembered, and a bubble of anger resurfaced—anger laced with pain.

Pain? Wait . . . what? My head hurt. I mean, it freaking killed. Like somebody had taken a pickax to my eyes. And why was I wet? I concentrated on my fingers, got them to obey me enough to brush against each other. They were soaked but warm. Why was the rain warm?

"Stay with me." There was the man's voice again, but this time it wasn't soothing. It sounded urgent, demanding.

My feet were cold. Shoes. I'd left them at Alex's house. No, Maddy had left *hers* at Alex's house. She had mine. She had my sweatshirt and coat, too; that was why I was so cold. At least I thought she did. I tried to look down, but my head wouldn't move. It was plastered in place.

It hurt to breathe. I pried my eyes open and saw the flashing lights. What had happened to my windshield? Was that a tree branch on my dashboard, and what was with the red paint coating the jagged pieces on the passenger-side window?

"Hurts," I choked out.

"I know." I turned toward the man but couldn't make out his face. It was blurred . . . hazy. "I'm going to give you something for the pain, but first, can you tell me your name?"

My name. My name? God, it hurt to think. I shook my head, the idea of having to formulate one single word was too much to bear. I saw a flash of metal to my right and tried to turn my head. They were cutting something; the sound of the metal blades hitting each other tore through my mind. Maddy's side of the car was dented in, dirt and leaves ground into the thousands of spiderweb cracks that laced the window.

I shivered as the frigid night air hit me. The passenger-side door was gone, two gloved hands tossing it aside in a hasty effort to get inside . . . to get to Maddy. Her body was slumped forward, resting at an odd angle against the dashboard. Hurried words, none of which I understood, echoed through the car as they gently eased her back against the seat, her head lolling to one side. Somebody reached for her neck and then her wrist before shaking his head and backing out of the car. If I had the strength to speak, I would've yelled at them to leave her be, to let her stay in the safe confines of the car, not to move her into the dark, wet night.

Maddy? I whispered in my mind. Her eyes were open and she was staring at me. Why didn't she blink? Why didn't she move?

She didn't fight, didn't cry out in pain when they pulled her out of her seat. She lay there boneless in their arms, a spot of wetness rolling off her cheek. I followed the drop of water to the floor and saw one of my shoes lying on the dirty floor mat by my phone. Where was the other?

"Stay with me," the man said. "Can you tell me your name?"

I didn't care about my name. I wanted to know where they were taking Maddy and why she looked so quiet and cold. I heard the man talking to me, demanding that I answer him. I blocked him out, focusing my energy on calling my sister back.

"Maddy," I whispered, hoping she'd hear me. Hoping she'd acknowledge me, say something, anything.

"There you go. Good. Now, do you know where you are?"

I tried to shake my head, but it hurt to move. "No," I managed to whisper.

"That's okay," he said. "We're going to move you now. You're going to be fine."

"Maddy," I repeated as his hands reached out for me. I didn't fight it this time. I didn't struggle to stay there despite his demands. I simply let go.

6

It hurt. It hurt to move. It hurt to think. It hurt to feel, but I did it anyway. I struggled for a sense of place, of time, but there were no familiar voices, only noise. Constant machinelike thrumming.

I was no longer cold. In fact, I was hot. Sweltering hot. Through my confusion, I could hear a beeping. I homed in on that rhythmic sound until I could count in time with the beats.

With each beep came a recollection, a flash so jumbled and terrifying that I screamed inside my head, begging to be set free. The rain, the spinning of the tires, and the smell . . . the caustic, burning smell of gas. The hail coating the road, blurring the lane lines. Me jerking the wheel. The screech of brakes. The tree and the sound of our panicked cries as the branch shattered the windshield.

I could still hear the music playing on the radio, the annoying jingle for the local car wash circling in my brain like a rusted-out hamster wheel. I wanted it to stop, wanted to claw out my ears, my burning throat, and my hiccuping mind with a spoon.

I tried to call for help, but no sound came out. My hands grasped at the empty air as I tried to pull myself from the memories, from the smell of blood and burned rubber and the sharp sting of glass shards embedded in my skin. I could feel my arms and legs. They were tight, as if someone had tied a rope around them and pulled, to be cruel.

Something snapped, my body and mind realigning themselves in one horrifying jolt. I found my voice and cried out, stuck in an imaginary world so vivid, so toxic, that I would have sworn it was real.

"Hey, calm down. You're alive. You're safe."

Oh thank God. I knew that voice. It was distantly familiar.

Blinking, I took in the room. I could move now, whatever had had me trapped inside my mind was gone. Cursing the dull ache in my head, I turned toward his words, his face blurring into view. I knew him, or at least, I knew I should know him. His eyes, his gentle tone, everything about him poked at something locked deep in my pounding head.

He'd pulled a chair up beside my bed and was sitting in it, his head cradled in his hands. His shoulders sagged and his hands shook. He was pale, and judging from the sunken quality of his eyes, I gathered he hadn't slept in days. Wait . . . days?

"Hey, beautiful. Welcome back," he whispered.

I reached to wipe my eyes, but a searing pain blasted up my arm. Black spots flashed across my vision. I could feel the tears streaming down my face, but I couldn't do anything about them. The boy placed a gentle hand over mine and used the other to wipe away my tears before kissing my forehead.

It didn't fix my vision completely. I blinked a few more times, hoping to clear the last of the shadows, but all that did was squeeze more tears out and down my cheeks. The machines, the call button on my bed . . . the entire room around me was off balance, and trying to focus on it made my head ache more.

The boy pulled back, and I searched his face for a spark of knowledge. I hoped he'd tell me his name, prayed he'd say *my* name. I desperately needed him to remind me who I was and why I was here.

"You scared me. You scared everyone. We thought we'd lost you," he continued. His eyes were glossy, and one tear managed to slip out before he blinked more of them back. Why was he crying?

I fought against the heavy fog settling over my body and moved my head, thinking for sure I would see someone else in the room. I clearly remembered two screams—one mine, one not—and eyes staring at me. But there was no other bed, no other girl, just a long windowsill and a small table on wheels, both of which were buried underneath flowers. Maybe it was a dream, a horribly vivid, warped dream.

I counted fifteen vases of flowers on the windowsill alone before I gave up and looked at the arrangement closest to me. It was sitting on the rolling table, the card tucked into a massive display of white roses.

The boy followed my line of sight. "Here," he said as he handed me the card. "They're from me."

I opened the envelope, not bothering to skim the handwritten message. What I wanted was to know who he was: Alex.

I turned that name over in my mind. It sounded familiar. I didn't know how or why, but it was a place to start.

"Alex." My voice cracked, and I had to swallow twice to accomplish that weak sound.

"Shh . . . relax. Don't try to talk," he said as he smoothed the hair off my face. "You broke some ribs and dislocated your shoulder, you hit your head pretty hard, too. They had to do surgery to set your wrist, but the doctors said it should be fine."

My eyes widened as I listened to him talk about my injuries, automatically thinking about the other girl, sitting in the car's passenger seat. I wondered if she was as banged up as me, if she was here, in the same hospital.

Turning my head, I saw the tubes, four of them in total, attached to me. I followed one to my finger, flexing my hand around the plastic device that held it trapped. There was one adhered to my chest, and one running into my nose. The last one was jammed into my arm.

When I blinked, I could feel a pull above my right eye. It stung more than anything. I guessed there was a bandage there, stitches maybe, but I would need a mirror to confirm. My left arm was heavy, like it was encased in bricks, and my wrist ached with a dull, throbbing pain that was bone deep.

Carefully, I reached my good arm behind me and tried to push myself up. My head spun, everything around me—the flowers, Alex, my own body—dissolving in a blur. My stomach churned, and I fought against the pain, swallowing hard to keep the bile-tinged water coming up my throat from spilling out.

Unwilling to move an inch, I frantically searched the room with my eyes. I needed a bathroom, a trash can, a plastic bag, anything to unload the contents of my stomach in. Alex noticed and shoved a small plastic bowl underneath my chin and grabbed for my hair. I didn't care about my hair or who was holding the bowl, I wanted the pain to end.

Alex didn't say a word as I heaved. He rubbed my back and reminded me to breathe. Easier said than done.

Carefully, he settled the pillows around me. The pain was receding, slowly leaving me with each passing breath. I found the vases on the windowsill again, my eyes moving from one to the next, counting as I went.

"You can stop counting," Alex said as he tossed the

paper towel he was using to dry his hands into the trash and took a seat next to me on the bed. "There are thirty-seven of them here, more at home."

I shook my head in confusion. How could I know thirty-seven people when I couldn't remember who I was?

"They're from our friends. Jenna, Keith, some of the guys on the soccer team. I think Coach Riley sent you some, too. Everyone's here, been camped out in the hall for the past two days."

I didn't recognize any of those people, and had he said *two days*?

I turned my head toward the hall windows, but the curtains were drawn, the door closed. There was a whiteboard stuck to the wall there, a bunch of numbers scribbled next to what I thought were times. Above it was my name. I think.

Maddy Lawton.

"Do you know where you are, what happened?" Alex asked. He looked worried, his eyes darting between mine and the whiteboard I was studying.

I shook my head. I could guess from the bed, the white walls, and the wires hooked up to me that I was in the hospital. I remembered being in an accident, a bad one. But who I was, how long I'd been here, and who the girl in the car *with* me was . . . yeah, that I had no idea.

"Do you know who you are?" His voice was barely a whisper, shaky and uncertain.

I looked up at the whiteboard again, then down to my

wrist. There was a plastic bracelet there with my name and a slew of numbers. "Maddy Lawton."

He smiled at my words. It was weak and tentative, but a confirmation that I was correct nonetheless.

"I'm Maddy." The whispered words felt foreign on my lips, but Alex nodded, the mere mention of my name lighting up his face. "Where is the other girl . . . the one that was in the car with me? Where is she? Is she okay?"

"Ella," Alex said, concern replacing the relief I'd seen in his eyes a moment earlier. "Your sister's name was Ella."

It sounded so simple, so perfectly right. "Ella."

"Maddy?" Alex was standing now, staring at me, waiting for me to do or say something. Problem was, I had no idea what that was. "Do you know who I am?"

I did, but not because I felt connected or drawn to him, rather because it was written on the card he'd shown me. Fear clawed its way through my system, the unnerving sensation that something was off . . . that I was off. It hit me, the realization that my entire knowledge base consisted of those two facts and nothing more. I knew who he was and who I was, but nothing more.

"You're Alex," I said as I stared down at his hand. It was locked in mine, his thumb gently tracing the lines of my veins. The touch was tender, soft, like the look in his eyes. Something you wouldn't do to someone you didn't know . . . really know. "And you're my boyfriend, right?"

My expression must have shifted because his next

words quickly tumbled out as if he was searching for the safe thing to say. "Everything's going to be okay, Maddy. You're gonna be fine. I'm gonna get your parents. They're outside in the hall, talking to your doctor."

"No, wait. Where's the other girl? My sister . . ." I had to pause, swallow down my pain to get those simple words out. "Where's Ella?"

I watched the lines of his face smooth out, his calm, soothing tone forced. "It's gonna be okay, Maddy. None of this is your fault."

My fault? "What? What do you mean *my fault?*"

He shook his head. The fact that he wouldn't explain was answer enough.

The brief silence that followed was all-consuming, and I slowly started to piece things together. I didn't hear the cry that escaped my throat, my mind too trapped in the shattering image of that girl . . . of Ella in the seat next to me, her blue eyes staring lifelessly at me as they pried her out of the car.

"Don't cry. Please, Maddy, don't cry. Nobody blames you. The roads were wet and the car slid. There was nothing you could do to stop it."

He reached out to me, and I moved back. "No! Don't touch me." I didn't want to be comforted or held. I wanted him to tell me what had happened, why I couldn't remember anything, *anything* except that girl's dead eyes.

7

Alex left me there sobbing, unable to form a coherent sentence. I saw the terror in his eyes when he finally got up and scrambled for the door. He had begged me to calm down, promised me everything would be fine. He was wrong, so wrong. Nothing would ever be *fine* again.

If what he was slowly trying to ease me into realizing was true, then the girl next to me in the car, the one I killed, was my own sister. Nothing . . . not the terrifying inability to remember who I was, not even the pain that was lancing through my head could compete with that dark truth.

"She's awake," I heard him say. The sound in the hall was deafening. Cheers mingled with cries. I saw a girl make for my door. I couldn't pull her name from the tattered recesses of my mind. Didn't need to because the swell of emotion that came from a glimpse of her face was more than enough. Hatred clawed at me, a complete and bone-deep hatred solely directed at her. Thankfully, Alex stopped her at the door and gently eased her aside to let someone in.

The door closed, blocking out the people in the hall, and the smell of coffee flooded the room. I looked up at the man, stared straight at him and prayed he would somehow make sense of this for me.

He stopped midstep and watched me. I prayed he would see the plea in my eyes, would say or do something to jar the simple recognition of who I was and what had happened back into place.

The man dropped his cup, black coffee covering his shoes as he stood there frozen for what seemed like an eternity. His shoulders shook, and it was then that I saw his tears. He didn't do anything to try to hide them. I swear I saw a brief flash of confusion cross his face, as if he were trying to see something that wasn't there, as if, like me, he was trying to fit what he'd been told into a box that wasn't the right size.

"Mr. Lawton?" It was Alex's worried tone that tore the man's eyes from mine. "She seems confused, like she's not sure who she is or why she's here. I know it's probably the pain meds they gave her—the doctor said she may be a bit hazy for a while—but she's asking questions about . . ." He drifted off, the pity I heard in his voice overwhelming. "I don't know what she remembers, and I thought . . . I didn't want to tell her . . . I thought maybe you and Mrs. Lawton . . ."

The older man's confusion disappeared, and he held up his hand for Alex to stop talking. He walked over to my bed and carefully sat down. His hand hovered for a second, trembling, before he wiped away my tears. "How's my sweet girl?"

I leaned into his hand, wondering how a simple gesture could bring me so much solace. "Why am I here? What did I do?" The questions flew from my mouth, each one calling forth more unease, more uncertainty.

"Everything is fine, Maddy. Your mother and I promise you that everything is going to be fine."

I winced at his words, the name Maddy tearing through me with such fury that I forgot to breathe. I would've gladly stayed that way, let the last breath of air leave my body as I withered away from the guilt that plagued me. A guilt I didn't understand. "Where's my sister?"

"She's gone, sweetheart." He tried hard to hide his pain, the glistening of tears I could see rimming his eyes, but I heard the hitch in his voice, the small shudder that accompanied those three heavy words.

My breath caught, setting off a whirl of high-pitched alarms. The first warning bell sounded, and Alex's face went pale. Dad was there, his hands hovering over me looking for some unknown hurt to soothe. My mother came barreling into the room, a doctor and two nurses close on her heels. One nurse went for the IV, the other to the machine attached to the wall. The doctor went for me. Mom pushed him aside.

"I won't lose you, Maddy." Her hands were on either side of my face, her eyes so close to mine that I could see the specks of gold hidden in the green. "Look at me. Look at me, Maddy!"

I did. I opened my eyes wide and stared at her. Anger, determination, maybe fear . . . I don't know what I saw, but the intensity of it speared me, kept my thoughts from lapsing into that dark space, and my eyes focused solely on her. "God already took one of my daughters. He can take anything else he wants from me, but not you, Maddy. *Never you.* Do you understand me? Now breathe!"

I did, not because I wanted to live, but because Mom told me to . . . She ordered me to. My breath hitched as I struggled to fill my lungs, and I gasped as the air burned its way down my throat.

The doctor circled around to the other side of the bed. He had my wrist in his hand as the nurse played with the dial on my IV. Mom ignored them all, completely focused on me.

"That's it, Maddy," Mom coaxed me, her calming tone encouraging me to live, her eyes demanding it. The pitch of the alarms slowly eased as I took one choking breath after another. Mom's voice echoed the sound, her tone becoming more soothing with each passing second.

She pulled me into her arms. I couldn't hear what she

was whispering past the dark question swirling in my head. I fought against her hold and turned. Dad was standing by the door, his hand braced on the wall. He looked like he was about to collapse. Alex had—he'd crumpled to the ground at my father's feet and was muttering something about letting Maddy live.

Everybody in this room adored me, had literally gone to pieces at the thought of me dying. But what about the other one? What about Ella? Who was with her when she died? Who was with her now?

8

It was quiet. The people gathered in the hallway had gone home yesterday afternoon, and the nurses who had been checking my vitals had eased back, coming in only when one of my alarms sounded, which was pretty much never. They wanted me to rest, or at least that is what they said, even offering to give me something to help me sleep. I didn't want to close my eyes, never mind sleep, but I took the meds anyway, hoping they would take me to a place my dreams couldn't reach. They didn't. The nightmares were always there, lurking, waiting for me to close my eyes and let go.

I rolled my head to one side, the scent of bleach and stale coffee stinging my senses. I'd grown used to it, actually found it comforting. It kept me grounded.

Blinking long and hard, I resumed my careful study of

the ceiling. It hadn't changed in the three gruesomely long hours I'd been staring at it. It was white, a large beige streak running down the center where there obviously used to be a divider. They must have taken two separate rooms and mashed them into one. It hadn't worked; the scar was still there for everyone to see.

A lone tear traced a path down my cheek. It felt good to cry when nobody was watching. Every time I woke up, Alex was there, holding my hand, assuring me that in a few days everything would be okay. I wished I had his faith.

Right now, he was sleeping in the chair next to my bed. Mom and Dad were there, too. They were sleeping, their bodies crammed onto the love seat in the corner. Dad looked worn, tense, his body fidgeting while he rested. I couldn't help but wonder if he was trapped in a series of nightmares like I was.

The door to my room scraped open and the night nurse walked in, surprised, I think, to see me awake. "Not tired?" she asked as she fiddled with the machine that tracked my vitals. "I can give you something else if you want."

"No," I said. Truth was, I was exhausted, more tired than I ever remembered feeling. But falling asleep, reliving the few details I could piece together, was destroying me.

"My sister. Ella," I whispered, hoping not to wake Alex or my parents. "Can you tell me anything about her? Was she even alive when they brought her in?"

The nurse's eyes darted toward my parents.

"They won't tell me," I said. I'd already asked them a thousand times. They kept shaking their heads, telling me not to think about that right now. I asked Alex during one of the rare moments my parents stepped out of the room. All he could say was that it wasn't my fault. As if that was somehow supposed to make me feel better, less guilty.

"Please, I need to know something. Anything," I continued.

"I don't work in the emergency room, so I don't know how much I can tell you."

"Can I see her? I mean, I know she's not . . ." I paused, unsure of how to explain the urgent need I had to see my sister. A sister I didn't remember having. "Please, I want to see her."

She wavered for a minute, her hand tapping nervously on the rail of my bed. "All right," she finally said, and I simultaneously felt relief and dread. I needed to do this. I wanted to do this, but the thought of coming face-to-face with what I'd caused had me wishing I'd never asked.

I sat up, wincing as my bare feet met the cold tile floor.

"Here," the nurse said. She handed me a pair of socks, but I pushed them away. I liked the chill, the jarring sensation reminding me that I was alive.

Alex heard the nurse's muffled words and stirred, his eyes opening as I stood up. "What's going on? You good?" he asked, his eyes darting between me and the nurse. "Why are you out of bed?"

I put my finger to my lips to shush him. "I'm good," I whispered. "She's gonna take me to . . ." I trailed off, unsure of how to explain the desperate need I had to see my sister or the overwhelming sense of loss that plagued me.

"She's gonna take you where?" Alex asked as he put his hand around my waist to keep me steady.

I lowered my eyes, then let the words fall from my lips. "To see my sister."

Alex's eyes widened in shock, his arm tensing around me as the color drained from his face. "What? Why? No."

He let go of me and turned to wake my parents. I stopped him. "Please, I don't want them there." *I don't even want you there,* I added silently.

"Maddy, listen to me. Seeing Ella won't bring her back. It will only make things harder for you, make it more real."

"It already is real," I said. "I miss her, Alex, and I don't know why. I don't remember anything about her. Not what her voice sounded like. Not what her favorite TV show was. Not even if she preferred chocolate or vanilla ice cream. All I know is that something inside me is missing, gone, and I need to see her to make sense of it."

I didn't expect him to understand. I didn't get it myself. But what I wanted, what I needed was for him to let me do this.

9

The nurse insisted on wheeling me down to the family viewing room that was attached to the morgue. I wanted to walk and went to tell her as much, but Alex picked me up before I got the chance and deposited me into the wheelchair, then pushed me toward the elevator himself.

I expected to be led into a dark basement room where the walls were lined with steel cubbies for bodies. I wasn't prepared for a quiet room with two metal chairs and an altar for praying. One of the orderlies wheeled in a metal gurney, the still body underneath it covered with a plain blue sheet. Funny, I thought the sheet would be white and starchy, and have PROPERTY OF CRANSTON GENERAL emblazoned on it, but I guess it didn't make a difference either way.

The orderly looked at me, then to Alex, before handing

the nurse a clipboard and a pen. She signed her name on the form, pausing once to check the time on her watch before logging it on the paper.

"Do you need anything else?" the guy asked, and I shook my head. "Then I will . . . uh . . . give you some privacy."

The room was silent. Too silent. The nurse was still there, tucked in the corner watching . . . waiting. I couldn't move, couldn't bring myself to get up from the wheelchair and take those few steps to where Ella's dead body lay. I had begged the nurse to bring me here, and now I wanted to leave.

"Maddy?" Alex questioned as he knelt in front of me. "You don't have to do this. Nobody expects you to do this."

I could hear the offer in his voice, the hope that I would change my mind and retreat to my hospital room and the promise of more mind-numbing drugs.

"I'm fine," I said as I got up and willed myself to take that first step and then another until I stood next to the steel bed, staring down at the impossibly still form.

"You ready?" the nurse asked.

I nodded and she reached for the corner of the sheet, easing it down to where my sister's shoulders met her neck. Even staring at the floor, I could feel her there, as if she was calling to me, daring me to look at her. My hands started shaking, my entire body drenched in a sweat that contradicted the chilled air of the room. I steeled my resolve, had to count to five three times before I found the courage to look up.

"Where are her clothes?" I don't know why I asked that. I knew her clothes were probably bloodstained and covered in glass. But I thought perhaps seeing them—the color, the brand, something as simple as whether she wore tank tops or bras would jar my memory and connect me to her in some way.

Alex shrugged. "Don't know. I guess they probably gave them to your parents."

"Do you know what she was wearing? Did you see her when they brought us in?"

"No," he said, and looked away. His answer was curt and filled with an anxious quality I hadn't heard from him before. I briefly wondered what he was hiding, what he was afraid to tell me. "Your clothes were gone by the time I got here. They'd cut everything off to get to your injuries."

I nodded. It made sense, I guess.

"She had one of her shoes on. Blue sneakers, I think, if that helps."

It did, actually. I could picture them. They were light blue with gray laces. There was writing on the side, like somebody had signed them with a black Sharpie. And comfortable. "What was I wearing?"

"Nothing. You left your shoes at my house. I found them on the lawn next to a chair. Why?"

"No reason," I said, and stared down at my sister. Her

eyes were closed, the skin surrounding them a dusty blue. Maybe it was bruising from the accident. More likely that's the way dead eyes looked.

Her lips were parted as if she were trying to say something, but no sound came out—not a whisper, not a weak breath. I could see her wounds, where her head had met with the shattered windshield, where a stray piece of glass had embedded itself in her shoulder. She was pale, ashen white, and her tangled hair was splayed across the steel, parts of it streaked with blood. But even like this, bruised and smeared with death, she looked exactly like me.

"I . . . me . . . we're the same." I choked out the words, and Alex hurried to my side. His entire frame shook next to mine as he looked down at the same dark reality. That could've been me. That should've been me.

"Of course," Alex said. "You're twins."

She didn't just look like me; I had a distinct feeling she *was* me. I ran my hand across the gash outlining her cheek. It cut across the bone, a jagged mark stretching to her ear. I tucked a darkened strand of hair behind her ear and bent down to kiss her cheek, to beg for forgiveness and promise that I'd keep her memory alive. That's when I saw them . . . the two tiny dots marring her right ear.

Without thinking, I reached for my own ear, running my finger across the earlobe, knowing what I'd find: *One* hole, *one* minuscule depression.

"What's wrong, Maddy?" Alex asked. When I didn't

answer, when I didn't so much as blink, he grabbed my hand and pushed me toward the door. He could drag me out of here, he could remove me from this room, from this hospital, from this world, and it still wouldn't stop the memories from flooding my mind.

My sister and I were thirteen and away at summer camp. It was the last year we went, the last year I remembered spending hours at night talking about anything and everything until the batteries of our flashlights died. The girl in the cabin next to ours was evil; in seventh grade she already was what Jenna would become in high school.

She'd been making fun of us for days. Apparently, one-piece bathing suits were for losers who chose to take art classes over sailing and volleyball. Didn't bother me—the total influence that girl had on my life would last two weeks, then I'd never have to see her again. But Maddy . . . she was peeved and wanted to prove that she was as good as, if not better than, that girl. Somehow, Maddy decided a second piercing in each of her ears was the way to do it.

Maddy handed me a needle from the sewing kit Mom had stashed in her trunks and an ice pack she'd snagged from the nurse's office. Everybody else in our cabin was asleep, had drifted off hours ago. We hadn't told them about our plan. This was our secret . . . a secret sisters would keep.

Maddy squinted, her eyes shut so tightly that her face scrunched up, making her look painfully amusing. I told her to relax, but she didn't. She grunted for me to get it over with, then dug her nails into the wooden frame of our bunk bed.

We were naïve back then and assumed five minutes with an ice pack would numb her ear enough for there to be no pain. I never did get to pierce the other ear; she swore and jumped the second I jabbed the needle through her skin.

"Jesus, Ella. That hurt," she yelled, and shoved me away.

Maddy made me swear to never tell Mom, and only wore an extra earring when we were at school. She stopped wearing the extra one altogether a few years back. The hole was nearly closed now, the pinprick-sized mark almost invisible.

I remembered her words clear as day. It was the first time she'd ever yelled at me, the first time she'd ever physically pushed me away. I also distinctly remembered her calling me Ella. *Me.* Ella.

Seeing my sister lying there on that steel table unlocked a piece of my mind I'd lost a few short days ago. A history, dreams, a future that belonged solely to me. They came back . . . every memory I ever had, hurtling to the surface. The My Little Pony lunch box I got the first day of kindergarten. The matching dresses we wore for Christmas each year until we were ten. The day we graduated from junior high—Maddy in heels, me in flip-flops. Josh arguing with the pizza guy last week over whether or not he should get his steak-bomb pizza for free because it took them more than thirty minutes to deliver it. And Maddy, yelling at me in the car because she thought I was a loser, someone to be ashamed of.

I turned my head toward the hallway, half-expecting my parents to walk through that door, to have somehow come to the same horrifyingly insane conclusion I had: that they were so completely wrong. That it was Maddy who was dead. That it was me—Ella—who had survived.

"Maddy, this was a bad idea," Alex said. "I shouldn't have let you do this, not without your parents here at least."

My parents. Mom was so excited when she realized Maddy was the one who had survived. Dad standing there next to her, immersed in the same joy. They didn't see me; they saw Maddy. Everybody saw Maddy.

"Josh?" He was the one person who knew me, who would see *me*. "Where's Josh? I want to talk to Josh."

Alex's hand tensed around mine, his eyes looking everywhere but at me. "He's at home, Maddy. After Ella . . . he's home."

"What?" That didn't make any sense. Josh and I had been inseparable since ninth grade. I had to kick him out of my house most Saturday nights, and he'd be back first thing Sunday morning with a new anime movie or some extra-credit project for physics. The only reason he wasn't at my house the night of the accident was because I'd kicked him out. I'd needed to finish my last sketch and the constant chiming of his phone with incoming texts from

Kim had been distracting me. But why wasn't he here now? "This doesn't make any sense. None of this makes any sense."

"He came to the hospital with me, Maddy, but by the time they got you settled into your room . . ."

"No, wait." The burning in my chest amplified and panic began to wash over me. I yanked on his hand until he stopped. I wasn't ready to leave. Not yet.

"Miss Lawton, we need to get you back upstairs," the nurse said. She stood up from her seat in the corner and grabbed the wheelchair I'd left sitting in the middle of the room. "I want to take your vitals and give you something to calm down."

I waved her off and took a step closer to Alex. I didn't want to sit down and be wheeled away. I wanted an answer. "Why did Josh leave? Why didn't he stay?"

Alex hesitated as if weighing his words. He started to step back, but I reached for his wrist, holding him in place. The tears had begun again, my body shaking with frustration over the truth that everybody refused to see. How could I make him understand that I was Ella? That the hand he was holding on to was not his girlfriend's but her sister's. Mine.

"Alex?" There was a demand in the nurse's tone, a plea to him to do something to calm me down, or she would.

"Don't worry about Josh," Alex said as he gently guided me into the wheelchair. "He knows it wasn't your fault."

Oh, it was absolutely my fault. I remembered everything

now, every last gruesome detail of how I'd killed my sister. My sobs echoed through the hall as he wheeled me onto the elevator, the sound so hollow, so pitiful, that I winced. But it wouldn't stop: not the tears, not the sobs, not the pain.

"Nobody blames you, Maddy. Nobody," he continued as the nurse leaned over to take my pulse. She looked worried, scared even. Alex looked like he was going to be ill.

I pushed the nurse away and turned toward Alex: "Look at me. Stop telling me it isn't my fault and look at me!"

He circled around to the front of my wheelchair and looked into my eyes. "I've been looking at nothing but you since the accident, Maddy, and I still see the same strong, beautiful girl I always have. This . . . what happened to your sister doesn't change that."

I couldn't help but wonder what he would say when he figured out that it was Ella and not his precious Maddy he was taking care of.

10

The elevator doors opened at my floor and Dad
rushed toward them at the sound of my cries. Mom was
there, too, hollering at Alex for not waking them up.

"Not Alex's fault," I managed to sob out. "Ella."

That last, heavy word took an enormous amount of
energy, and I felt myself slipping, my mind closing in on
itself.

"Maddy?" Alex said, the fear I felt pouring off him ri-
valing my own. I didn't want to see the hope in their eyes
die as I forced them to realize that I was Ella.

I studied my dad, my own father, the man who I'd had
breakfast with every day for the past seventeen years. The
man who coached my middle school soccer team. The man
who tried to teach me how to ride a bike one afternoon
when I was seven and sat with me in the ER later that
same day as they splinted my sprained wrist. Years of time

together . . . of experiences, and my own father didn't even recognize me.

Or maybe he didn't want to. Maybe he wanted it to be Maddy who had lived, so that was who he saw.

Horror flashed through his eyes as he took the wheelchair from Alex and pushed me into my room. Distantly, somewhere in the remote crevices of my mind, I remembered that he still thought I was Maddy and that the soothing words he whispered weren't meant for me.

"What were you thinking?" Mom had Alex by the collar of his shirt and was yelling at him. "Why would you let her go down there? Why didn't you wake us?"

"Please. He didn't do this. I did," I protested.

Realization of who I was and what I needed to tell them set in. I started to shake, every inch of my body freezing. *Cold.* I tried so hard to say the words, to tell my parents I was Ella, but I couldn't get a sound past my lips.

Dad helped me out of the wheelchair and back into bed, then sat down next to me. "We're gonna get you through this, Maddy. I promise."

Get through this? The phrase sounded so foreign to me, an unattainable solace that I had absolutely no right to hope for. I had been tired and angry and jealous that things came so easy for her. I'd screamed at her. The last words I said to her, the last words she would ever hear came from me, and they were bitter and mean.

"What have I done? Oh my God, what have I done?" I wanted nothing more than to trade places with Maddy, to give her back the life I'd taken. I didn't want to be here. Not without her.

"We are not angry with you, baby girl. We could never be angry with you."

Dad never called me that. He called me Bellsy when I was a kid or Isabella when I was in trouble, but mostly he called me Ella. Baby girl was Maddy's nickname, one she both hated and used to her advantage when she wanted a curfew extension or extra money for shoes or a new pair of jeans.

"I'm so sorry, I didn't mean for her to die." I shrank backward, the weight of those words settling deep in my core. Pressing my aching shoulders deeper into my pillow, I wished, for a moment, that I could dissolve into the bed and never come back.

"We know that," Mom said. "It was a terrible accident, but you are here with us, Maddy. You're alive and you have your whole life ahead of you. Your whole life. I want you to think about that, concentrate on getting stronger. That's what your sister would want."

I looked at Dad, wondering if he felt the same way, if he believed that, too. He smiled and nodded, but I could see the anguish behind his eyes, the battle he was waging to keep his emotions in check. "Ella wouldn't want you to waste a single minute of your life feeling guilty. She'd want you to live, to do everything you ever dreamed of and more. Do it for her, Maddy. Live for her."

They wanted me to be Maddy. Alex, Dad, Mom, the

74

friends who had waited in the hall for hours . . . days until I woke up, only leaving when Alex promised to call them if my condition changed. Every single one of them wanted Maddy to live. That was who they thought I was, that was who they told themselves I was. Maybe the real problem here wasn't that they didn't recognize me, maybe it was that I was me and not my sister. How was I supposed to tell them the truth, the horrible truth—that the girl they had rallied around, had begged God to let live, was gone?

I couldn't do it to them. I couldn't do it to her. If they wanted Maddy to live, then I'd make sure she did. Maddy deserved a chance at a real life, at happiness. I'd taken that from her with one angry jerk of the wheel. In my own selfishness, I'd done this to her, cut her life short. She'd get the life she deserved. She'd grow up, go to college, and have a family. I'd make sure she had everything she ever wanted or die trying. I'd make this up to her, to my parents, to Alex. I'd bury myself and give Maddy my life in return.

11

It was freezing out. A thin layer of frost glistened on the granite headstones as people carefully picked their way across the slick grass. It was supposed to warm up and be bright and sunny by midafternoon. Didn't matter to me either way.

The inside of the car smelled like a combination of rug shampoo and pine trees, and I couldn't help but wonder if there was a cheap cardboard air freshener hanging from the rearview mirror. If I tried, I could probably see it from here. But that'd mean I'd actually have to move, and I didn't want to.

The windows had fogged over, and I swiped my hand across the glass. Mom and Dad were already there, standing by the giant hole in the ground and talking with the minister. People filled in around them, their heads bowed and their shoulders tense.

I was glad to be out of the hospital, doing something besides staring at the white walls while everybody talked in hushed tones about how much progress I'd made. I was no longer crying and hadn't taken a pain pill in days, but that had little to do with "progress" and everything to do with me not caring anymore. Part of me had died with Maddy, a piece so significant, so integral to who I was that I felt completely lost without her.

The shrink they'd sent to talk to me in the hospital thought it'd be a good idea if I went to the burial. Something about closure and moving on. My doctor agreed and discharged me a day early so I could attend. I'd said I'd go, but now that I was here, I couldn't move from the car, couldn't walk ten yards to the graveside to see my sister . . . to see *myself* buried.

The car door opened, and I slid over to avoid the rush of cold air.

"You coming?" Alex asked.

I'd been in the hospital for twelve days and he was there the entire time, hovering, always asking me if I wanted something to drink or if my shoulder hurt. At first I thought it was sweet. I enjoyed his company over my dark thoughts. But now I felt suffocated. I needed some privacy to say goodbye to my sister, to apologize for the last words I'd said to her. But I was never alone. Alex was always there.

He offered me his hand and I took it, stared at it as I memorized every minute detail, every insignificant flaw as his fingers entwined with mine. "Where's your coat?" he asked as he helped me out of the car.

"At home," I said.

My parents were paranoid about bringing me out into the cold and had thrust two coats on me when they picked me up from the hospital this morning. Truth was, I didn't want either one. Something about the slap of the cold air against my skin felt good, reassuring. Each goose bump that rose on my skin was welcome, a sharp reminder that despite the misery I was encased in, I was, in fact, still alive.

Besides, the two wool coats weren't mine; they were Maddy's. I'd worn her black dress, but having her coat surrounding me, her warmth seeping into me, seemed wrong.

"Here," Alex said as he shrugged out of his. I turned to let him wrap it around me, flinching when his hand brushed against my neck. Up until now, the only part of my body he'd touched was my hands.

"Your shoulder hurt?" he asked. They'd reset my dislocated shoulder while I was unconscious. My arm was still in a sling, but that was mostly due to the weight of the cast on my left wrist.

"No, it doesn't hurt. Your hands are just cold."

He warmed them with his breath before turning the collar of his coat up around my neck. There were four white chairs facing the coffin, like sterile beacons directing me home. I didn't want to sit in one. I didn't want anybody's focus on me. I wanted to fade into the background and watch from a distance as I made peace with my decision to become my sister.

Mom motioned for me to take the one beside my dad, and I sat down, felt the legs of the white folding chair sink into the wet ground under my weight. Alex took the seat next to me, his hand never leaving mine. Dad sat on the other side, his eyes meeting mine as he patted my hand.

"You doing okay?" Dad asked.

Not knowing how to answer, I shrugged. I was so far removed from okay that I couldn't even put a name to the mess of emotions I was feeling. Anger, pain, regret, and an overwhelming amount of guilt churned together, leaving me numb.

"It's going to be fine, Maddy," Dad said, uttering the same reassuring words he had each morning as he left the hospital to go home and change. "We'll get through this, I promise. So long as we still have you, we can get through this."

I hadn't seen Dad cry since that first day in the hospital, but he looked fifteen years older than I remembered. His suit was impeccable and his shoes polished, but the wrinkles around his eyes were a little too deep, his voice a little too raspy. Mom was quiet, had been since that night the nurse and Alex took me to see Maddy. Her eyes were red and her hands trembled. She caught me watching her and mouthed that she loved me as she reached across my father to smooth my hair. I did my best to smile, every broken piece of me becoming a little more jagged with the knowledge that their love was not for me, but for Maddy.

Not able to look Mom in the eyes, I turned toward the gathering crowd. I wanted them to hurry up and leave, for this whole thing to be over so I could go home and be alone.

The chairs had been set up in a semicircle, my parents and Alex and I seated at the front, my grandparents behind us. From where I sat, I could see nearly everybody, could feel their eyes watching me. Looking around, I spotted my cousins and my aunts. One uncle was quietly telling his kids to stop poking at each other. There were neighbors, our childhood babysitter, and a handful of guys from Dad's office. I could even pick out the women from Mom's book club. None of them bothered me. It made sense for them to be here, supporting my parents. It was the crowd behind them that had me squeezing Alex's hand to the point of pain.

I'd figured Jenna would come. She was Maddy's best friend and spent as much time at our house as Alex did. The rest—the field hockey team, the boys' soccer team, the two dozen kids who'd never looked twice at me before today—they bothered me.

"What are they doing here?" I asked Alex.

Alex looked confused. "What do you mean what are they doing here? It's your sister's burial service, Maddy. Why wouldn't they be here?"

"They don't know m—" I paused, swallowed hard, and

corrected myself. "They didn't know Ella. I mean, with the exception of Jenna, I don't think any of them said more than two words to her. None of them. Ever."

"That doesn't mean they don't care."

"Yes, it does," I fired back, remembering how Jenna kindly asked me to drive myself to school our sophomore year because being seen with me wasn't *good* for Maddy.

"They don't care about Ella. They never have!"

Alex wasn't one to swallow his own words, but I watched him do it, felt his hand twist in mine as he struggled to stay calm. "They are not here for her. They came for you, Maddy. You."

"For me? For *me*?"

I tried to hold on to my anger. If I wasn't careful, I'd slip, let my own voice seep into my words. I blinked long and hard, then shook my head. Not here. I wouldn't lose it here.

Mom looked at me, indecision and pity warring in her eyes. The minister had stopped talking and was looking at my father for guidance. Everybody else . . . well, they were staring at me. They'd heard my rant, heard me tear up Alex's friends at my own burial.

My vision blurred, the whole world narrowing down to one gaping, black hole in the earth. The grave. *My* grave. I searched the crowd, looking for some way to escape. Jenna took a step toward me, but Alex waved her off. He leaned in and whispered something in my ear, my dad following suit on the other side. I don't know what either of them said; it was nothing more than jumbled words in a sea of white noise.

The second my eyes caught Josh's, I could breathe. It was as if something familiar in me clicked into place, and for the first time in over a week, I felt like me. He wasn't wearing his standard Mountain Dew T-shirt and ratty jeans. He had on a black suit and tie and what looked like uncomfortable shoes. I liked him better in T-shirts and jeans.

Kim was standing next to him, with the rest of the anime club behind them. They were shuffling their feet, looking everywhere but at me, as if itching for this whole thing to end.

Josh's eyes met mine with an intensity I didn't quite understand. He'd never looked at me like that—with such unadulterated hatred. His eyes were red, but the sheen of tears couldn't hide his feelings.

Kim reached for him and whispered something in his ear. He brushed her off and took a step farther away. I thought he was going to leave, but he didn't. He shrank into the back of the crowd where he didn't have to look at me. She followed him, tried again to tell him something before handing him a tissue. Josh took it and twisted it in his hands until it resembled confetti. I fought the urge to go over and still his hands, to throw my arms around him and thank him for being one of the few people who was here for me . . . for Ella.

"Maddy, sweetheart," Dad said, his hand on my shoulder drawing my attention to him. "Why don't you let Alex or your grandmother take you home? I know the doctor thought being here would—"

"No," I said, cutting him off. I had every intention of staying, surrounded by people who couldn't care less about me as I absorbed the details of my life being memorialized, then buried away. "I'm fine. I want to stay."

Mom caught the edge in my voice and leaned across Dad to stare at me. She wasn't angry or embarrassed by my outburst, she was . . . wary. Maddy never snapped at them. She'd cry, plead, and give them the silent treatment until they cracked, but she never snapped. The one who snapped was me. That was Ella.

"Maddy?" Mom's eyes roamed every inch of my body looking for something I knew she wouldn't find.

The only way my parents were able to tell us apart as babies was a small freckle I had above my right eye. That night in the hospital after I'd woken up and had no idea who I was, I caught Mom carefully peeling away the bandage. She thought I was asleep, and I didn't do anything to tell her otherwise. At first I figured she was counting my stitches or checking to make sure they weren't infected. It wasn't until hours later, after I realized who I truly was, that I figured out what she'd been doing, why she ran her fingers gently across my stitches. She was looking for that identifying mark, a telltale sign that would confirm who I was, who she wanted me to be. But Maddy's face had been cut up when she hit the windshield and . . . well, I now had seven stitches where that freckle once was. She could stare at that tiny spot forever; the freckle wasn't there.

"I'm sorry," I said. "It's . . . I'm sorry."

At a nod from my mother, the minister continued, and everybody went back to studying their shoes. I didn't make another sound, not even a sob as my mother said her last goodbyes to the coffin, turned, and walked away.

I didn't move from my seat, didn't acknowledge the pitiful stares directed my way or my father's whispered words that it was time to go. I knew my way home; I'd get there eventually.

12

I didn't move until the last shovelful of dirt hit level ground. I was distantly aware of Alex watching me. He'd left me there at my insistence so I could make peace with what I'd done, say goodbye to my sister alone and in my own way. With her, I'd buried myself—every memory of who I was now—six feet under with the sister I'd put there.

The last of the cemetery crew left, and I stood up, searching my dress pocket for the things I'd taken from the hospital. "I'm so sorry," I said as I dug a small hole in the freshly turned dirt with the toe of my shoe. I'd read Alex's card a thousand times since he handed it to me. I knew he loved her, would do anything to keep her safe, and I'd do the same . . . for Maddy.

"I'll take good care of him," I said as I buried the card, praying that wherever she was, she could hear me, could forgive me. "He loves you. I mean, I guess I always assumed he did, but watching him these past couple of weeks . . . well, he does."

Tears burned behind my eyes. I'd hid them through the service, hadn't trusted myself to keep playing my part if I gave in to my emotions. But now, with nobody watching, I finally let them fall.

For the last few days, it had seemed like every memory I had of us as kids, every mundane detail consumed me. It was as if I was afraid that if I didn't catalogue everything from the exact date we got braces to the color of her toothbrush, then it would be lost, tiny pieces of her forgotten forever. I couldn't let that happen.

"Here, I brought this for you." I held a small flashlight in my hand. It was Alex's. He had used it in the hospital to study at night when I was sleeping. I'd taken it before I left, intent on burying it with Maddy.

"I meant to put it in the casket, but it was already closed," I said as I laid it on top of the dirt mound. I quickly swiped at the tears streaming down my cheeks, but it was no use. "Remember how we used to play hide-and-seek at Grandma's house?" I thought of the cobwebbed basement and dingy attic our cousins were always hiding in. We played together on the holidays as Mom did the dishes and Dad caught up with siblings he only saw twice a year.

When we were five, I hid in the laundry room closet and Maddy was in Grandma's dryer. She had the door cracked open enough so she could see, but I doubted that would give her away. No one ever thought to check the dryer.

I heard my cousin Jake laughing, that annoying cackle that meant he was about to do something mean. But that didn't surprise me; he was always mean. The sound got louder, and I tensed as I waited for him to find me. But it wasn't me he was after, it was Maddy.

Her cry sent me barreling out of the closet, fists balled and ready to hit Jake. He'd found her, but instead of yelling it to the rest of us, he'd kicked the dryer door shut and was pressing his entire weight against it, closing her in. It wasn't the small, cramped space that scared Maddy. It was the dark. Maddy was deathly afraid of the dark. Still was.

"Let her out," I demanded. She was banging on the door, her cries tearing through my heart.

"Make me," he taunted, and leaned further into the door, blocking my path to Maddy.

She'd stopped sobbing by then, her cries dissolving into muffled whimpers as she pleaded with Jake to open the door. I went to move around him, to push him out of the way and get to Maddy, but Jake was older and seemed twice my size. He shoved me hard, and I fell backward onto the tile floor.

I hit the closet-door handle on the way down. No blood or anything, but I remembered the bump and, later, Mom asking me a million questions like, was I tired and did I feel sick. Funny, I could still almost feel it—the pain that is, like my mind was triggering my body to recall every detail I could.

"I hate you," I had yelled at Jake as I scrambled to my feet. That was my sister . . . that was a part of me he had trapped in there.

"Ooh . . . Ella hates me. I'm sooo scared now," he teased back.

"Let her out or I'll get my mom."

"Gonna run to tattle to your mommy? What's the matter, Ella? Your sister's afraid of the dark?"

He knew she was. That's why he always hid in the attic. That's why he always won.

I may have only been five, but I had on dress shoes, hard patent-leather ones. And they were pointy at that. I was going for his knee, but my balance was off and I was angry, so angry that my foot flew higher.

Jake fell sideways to the ground and curled up in a ball, his face pale and his eyes watering. The sound that came out of his mouth was awful—low, guttural, and filled with pain. But now it was my turn to taunt him, my chance to remind him not to mess with Maddy. "Maddy is my sister," I said. "You leave her alone."

Maddy tumbled from the dryer and ran into my arms. Her face was red and blotchy, and she was gasping through her tears.

"Mom!" Jake yelled from the bathroom floor.

"Who's the baby now?" I teased. "Look who's calling his mommy for help now."

My aunt Helen came running up the stairs, my mom a few steps behind. Aunt Helen dropped to the floor, looking for some wound to soothe on her precious Jake. He couldn't speak, couldn't find the strength through his pain to tell her what I'd done.

"What happened?" Mom asked.

"Ella . . . kicked me . . . in . . . the balls," Jake rasped out, and Maddy giggled. Her giggle brought a quick smile to my face. If she was laughing, then it meant she was okay.

"Isabella Anne Lawton—" my mom started in, but I cut her off. I wasn't going to take the blame. Jake had it coming.

"He locked Maddy in the dryer and wouldn't let her out!"

Jake got hauled home without dessert, and I couldn't watch TV that night. Maddy . . . well, getting stuck in the dryer was punishment enough for her giggling as Jake rolled around on the floor, groaning in pain. Needless to say, Jake was never much interested in playing hide-and-seek with us after that Thanksgiving. In fact, he'd never much wanted to have anything to do with us since then. Fine by me. It was twelve years later and I still wasn't ready to forgive him.

"You think Jake is still bent out of shape about the dryer incident?" I joked as I toyed with the small thread that had come loose from the hem of my dress. I knew full well he was away at college, but the thought of him still being afraid of me and my pointy shoes brought a little bit of happiness to an otherwise sucky day. "Maybe that's why he didn't come to the burial? Well, anyway, I brought you a flashlight. I know it's probably dark in . . ."

I stepped back, shaking my head. What I was saying was insane. Maddy didn't care about the dark anymore. She was dead, wouldn't know if it was dark. But I knew it didn't matter how much white satin they lined your coffin with. Once the lid was closed, it'd be horrifyingly dark. Once the coffin was lowered six feet and covered with dirt, it would be suffocating and dark. And I'd done that to her. I'd put her there.

I fell to my knees and let my hands sink into the loose dirt. I'd taken the one thing . . . the one person I loved most in the world and destroyed her. "I didn't mean any of those things I said to you in the car. You were right; I'm the selfish one. And I'm not sick of your crap. I never was. I wanted you to talk to me, for it to be like it used to be when we were little, when I'd kick boys in the balls because they teased you."

I picked up a fistful of dirt and crushed it in my hands, watched as it fell between my fingers to the cold, damp ground. Everything was slipping away because of me.

"Oh God, what have I done!" I didn't fight the sobs that racked my body. I let them take over me, knowing that the pain and guilt I felt were nothing compared to what I'd done to Maddy. "I didn't mean for this to happen. I'd change places with you if I could, put myself in that grave if it meant you could live."

"Don't say that," Alex said as he knelt in the dirt next to me. He'd heard my last cry and had come over to try to drag me away from a reality I couldn't change. "Don't ever say that."

"But it's true. You don't understand how true it is."

"No, it's not. You feel that way now, but it will get better. I promise you, I'll make it better."

"How? How can anybody make this better?"

Alex stood up, his eyes distant, as if he was trying to find the appropriate thing to say. "I don't know, Maddy, but I will."

He held out his hand to me, his eyes tracking to a tree a few yards away. I knew Josh was there, knew he'd been watching me since I first stepped out of the car, knew he'd seen me break down and mourn for the sister who'd been his best friend.

"Come on," Alex said as he took my hand in his. "Let's get you home."

"What about him?" I asked, nodding toward Josh.

"I talked to him. He's good. I think he's waiting for us to go so he can say goodbye to Ella in private."

Say goodbye to Ella . . . say goodbye to me. I should've gone over there, told Josh I was sorry, but I didn't. Instead, I turned and walked straight into my new life.

13

I'd watched nearly every Netflix movie available for streaming and was seriously contemplating DVR'ing bad reruns of *The Brady Bunch* to keep my mind off what I had to do tomorrow. I intended on keeping the promise I'd made to my sister—my life was hers; I owed her that much. But playing Maddy for my parents and Alex was easy. They were forgiving. Any little mistake I made, they explained away as the result of my grief or pain meds. But playing her in front of six hundred random kids . . . that I hadn't thought through.

My bedroom door opened, and I tossed aside the remote as I tried to pull myself out of the sea of blankets Mom had tucked around me. It was hard, my shoulder protesting every move. I finally gave up and sank back down to the bed.

Alex chuckled at my clumsy movements and dropped

the new movie he had in his hand onto the bureau. It was the twelfth one he'd rented this week. My nightmares had gotten worse, each dream morphing into a hell I couldn't unsee. He'd stay as late as he could, watching movies or doing his homework. But eventually he'd have to leave, and I'd slip into the world where my dreams and reality collided into one terrifying truth.

"You worried about tomorrow?" Alex asked as he stripped three layers of blankets off my legs and helped me sit up.

Worried didn't quite cover it. I'd been hiding in the house, in this room for nine days, and it was time to become Maddy for the rest of the world. "No. I'm good."

"I talked to Jenna earlier. She said she called you again today, but you didn't pick up."

She'd called five times actually, and no, I hadn't picked up. I hadn't seen her since the burial, and even then it was from a distance. In the hospital, the doctors and nurses had kept everybody away, and I made sure the family-only visiting rule extended to Alex and nobody else.

"I know you guys had a fight that night at my party," Alex continued. "But that was nearly a month ago. Don't you think it's time to let it go? She has."

Jenna was the one person in my sister's life who I wanted no involvement with. If an argument at that party gave me a way out of the friendship, then I would take it. "It's been twenty-one days and sixteen hours since the accident, to be exact, and no, I'm not ready to give it up."

Alex sighed and shook his head. We'd had this same quiet disagreement every day since I got home, and I'd yet to budge. "She is having a tough time right now. Things aren't getting any better for her at home."

I tossed him a sideways glare. Things weren't so great around here either. To be honest, I was drowning in a hell of my own making. But you didn't see me complaining to everybody. "So why is that my problem?"

"I get that you're upset, but you know how Jenna—"

I held up my hand to stop him. I didn't want to talk about Jenna or how I was supposed to play nice with her. I was already freaked out about going to school tomorrow. Having him remind me that Jenna was going to be a constant fixture at my side was not helping. I needed to switch topics, and fast, before I changed my mind about everything.

"I don't want to talk about Jenna," I said. "I'll see her tomorrow. I'll see everybody tomorrow."

"Okay," Alex said as he stretched out next to me on the bed and reached for the remote. "But I don't get why you're avoiding her. She's your best friend, maybe she can help."

She was Maddy's best friend, not mine. I'd left *my* best friend standing at my sister's grave without so much as an apology. "I don't need her help. I have you."

"That you do."

He inched closer, his breath mingling with mine. I closed my eyes. I knew this was coming, that eventually he'd make a move, but I still wasn't prepared. I didn't want to sleep with him. I didn't even want to kiss him.

His lips had barely brushed mine before I pulled back, my heart pounding. I opened my eyes and stared down at my trembling hand pushing at his chest.

He saw it too and pressed his hand over mine, stilling the tremor. "Relax, Maddy."

I nodded, unsure what else to do. I'd promised my dead sister I'd give her the life she didn't get a chance to live, sacrifice my own dreams so that I could live hers. I loved her, would do anything for her, but not this. Not him.

Alex leaned in again, his careful approach exaggerated as I analyzed his every move.

"Relax," he whispered again, and I willed myself to try, focused on counting to twenty in my head.

"I love you," he murmured as his hands found their way to my back.

I tried to relax, to follow his lead, but I couldn't. "Don't," I said, and shoved him away.

Alex didn't have to say a thing. The disappointed way in which he unwound himself from me told me what I needed to know.

I knew what he was thinking and prayed my words would be enough. "Everything's different now. I can't . . . it's not . . . just no," I stammered out, completely incapable of coming up with a plausible excuse for why I suddenly wanted nothing to do with him.

Alex slid back on the bed, keeping one of my hands

locked in his. "You and me...the way you feel about me...is that what you mean?"

"No." I shook my head, hoping my weak smile was enough to reassure him. Then I spoke the same words I'd heard Maddy say to him a thousand times: "I love you. Always have."

"Always will?" he asked, that spark of life returning to his face.

"Yes." That was the one thing I was a hundred percent sure of. Maddy loved Alex. Always had, always would.

"Then what is it?"

I shrugged. "I don't know. It's different now. I'm different now." Different in that I wasn't Maddy and had never loved Alex. Different in that all these things—this room, this bed, the pictures tucked into the mirror, the boyfriend sitting next to me—weren't mine.

Alex tilted his head, the silent question *How?* reflected in his eyes. I took a deep breath and held it, searched for the courage to speak my greatest fears out loud. "I'm different now. I'm not the same girl I was before the accident. Not even close."

Alex smiled, not the sarcastic grin I was expecting, but one of quiet understanding. "You're nervous."

It wasn't a question, but I nodded anyway.

"We've done this hundreds of times, Maddy. Literally hundreds."

"I know." Maddy and Alex had spent the better part of our junior year with their lips locked together and served their fair share of time in detention for getting caught kissing in the hall. And if the accidental glimpse I'd got of Maddy's diary was correct, then they'd spent most of their summer rolling around in bed, or in the backseat of his Jeep, or on the beach, or . . . "I'm sorry, but I can't. Not yet."

He flashed me a grin and settled into the bed next to me. "I'll tell you what, we'll take it slow. It's Sunday, right?" I nodded, and he went on. "So, tonight we can hold hands. Next week we'll give kissing another try, and by the week after that, you should be good to go. What do you say? Sound like a plan?"

I nodded. That gave me two weeks to try to figure something out. Two short weeks, but at least it got me off the hook for tonight.

14

I spent an hour standing inside my sister's closet after Alex left and another twenty minutes this morning. It didn't matter what I put on, nothing felt right. Sweatpants and T-shirts had been my outfit of choice for the past few weeks, but I couldn't exactly wear those to school. Not if I was going to be Maddy.

My inspiration came not from my own wisdom, but from a picture Maddy had tucked in the corner of her mirror: her and Alex at the Fall Festival the week before the accident. She was beautiful, amazingly so, and I wondered why I'd never seen it until now.

I took that picture with me into the closet and went about assembling the exact same outfit—low-riding jeans and a wide brown belt that barely fit through the loops. Squinting at the picture, I tried to figure out which of three nearly identical gray hooded sweaters she had on. It was a closer peek at her hands that gave it away—the sleeves of the top had holes for her thumbs. I added a second long shirt, a pair of boots, an ugly scarf, and I was good to go. I was dying of heat, suffocating under the layers, but after one more quick scan of the picture, I was confident that I was dressed exactly like her.

Hair and makeup . . . well, that was a different story. I didn't have the slightest idea where to begin. Luckily, my left wrist was still in a cast. I could blame my less-than-perfect appearance on my inability to pull my lid taut with my left hand as I applied my eyeliner.

I wrapped the scarf around my neck one more time, pausing to breathe in her scent. The smell of her perfume mingled with a slight hint of Alex enveloped me, and for a second it was like she was there, giving me a hug. I missed everything about her—the way she smelled, the way she yelled at me for leaving my wet towels on the bathroom floor or using her crazy-expensive shampoo. I missed the amusement in her eyes when Dad told his lame jokes at dinner and the way she'd quietly poke her head into my room every night before she went to bed. Being surrounded by her clothes, her smell, her life made the heartache of losing her nearly unbearable.

The door nudged open, Bailey's nose inching in, pulling me from my memories. "How do I look?" I asked. He whined and lay down in the doorway. He'd been doing that since I got home—following me around, nudging my hands or my legs, begging me to acknowledge him. When nobody was looking, I would bury my head in the fur at his neck and remind him that I was still me.

"Come here, Bailey." I bent down and clapped my hands, hoping he'd finally enter Maddy's room. But he never did. He'd sit at the doorway and beg for me to come out, sometimes bark, but never once did Bailey come in. Probably because Maddy had trained him to stay out of her room by hurling her shoes at him if he so much as put one paw across the threshold. She hated my dog, claiming he smelled like dirt and slobbered too much. He did, but that's why I loved him.

"Treat?" I asked, and Bailey stood up, ears pointing forward. He stood there for a second, then turned around, walked into my old room, and climbed up onto my bed. Lucky him.

"He still won't come in?" Mom asked. She was staring at Bailey as he circled my bed looking for a comfortable spot to sprawl out.

"Nope. But I don't know why I care," I quickly added. Mom had been watching since I got home and had made more than one curious comment about why he was following me around. "He was Ella's dog, not mine. I feel bad for him. He misses her."

"That's why you care, because he's Ella's dog?"

Mom and Dad had been trying to get me to talk to them for days, thought I needed to open up, that I couldn't start to heal until I did. That's what her question was, an opening for me to walk through. I wouldn't.

When I stayed silent, Mom sighed and came into my room. "You sure about this?" she asked as she handed me an apple—which I presumed was supposed to be breakfast—and the doctor's note excusing me from gym for the foreseeable future. I also had a note I was instructed to hand to any teacher or administrator who questioned my prolonged absence. I doubted I'd need it. Everybody, including the principal, knew why I'd been out.

"Yeah, I'm sure. I want to go back. I need to go back."

I grabbed the apple from her hand and headed for the kitchen. She was following me, her quiet footsteps echoing behind me on the stairs. I took a quick glance at the fridge, briefly wondering if I was supposed to pack a lunch. Hmm . . . I didn't remember Maddy standing in the lunch line, but then again, I never saw her toting around an ugly brown paper bag either. Crap, it was barely seven in the morning and I was already stumbling.

"You hungry?" Mom asked. "I can fix you something to eat if you want." She looked confused and mildly optimistic that I'd say yes.

I was starving and wanted nothing more than a stack of pancakes with a side of sausage, but I didn't have time. Plus, I hadn't seen Maddy eat anything pork-related since middle school. "Nah, I'm good."

I grabbed my keys off the counter and headed out the door. "Remember to be home by six," Mom called after me. "I made an appointment for us to see the therapist tonight. You've been so . . ."

"Quiet? Closed off? Different?" I supplied when she struggled to find the right word. I'd always been those things. Problem was, I was no longer me. "I'm fine, Mom. We already had this conversation. I don't want to talk to somebody about what happened. I want to forget it and go on."

"We discussed this, Maddy. You're—"

"No, we didn't," I said, cutting her off. The last thing I was going to do was let some shrink go mucking around in my lie. I was having a hard enough time keeping it together as it was. "*You* said you wanted me to see a therapist. I never agreed to go."

"Maddy, sweetheart, your father and I met with the doctor. He thinks we need to come in as a family, try to work our way through this so that . . ."

"Work our way through this?" I could hear my voice climbing with each syllable. I didn't need to talk about it. I relived it every night. My hands crushing the steering wheel. The smell of pine and dirt as the branches shattered the windshield. The blood trickling down Maddy's face. Her dead eyes staring at me from the passenger seat. Those images were my constant bedtime companions.

"You want to know what I need?" I asked. "I need *everyone* to stop talking about it, stop making me think about it. I want to go to school, go watch field hockey practice, and then come home. I can't fix what happened. I would if I could. I'd trade my life for hers, gladly put myself in that grave so she could have her life back, but I can't. And I don't see how meeting with a shrink is going to help!"

Not wanting to listen to her reply, I slammed the car door closed. I didn't want to see the anguish in her eyes, hear the concern lacing her voice. And I didn't want her to see me cry. I couldn't pull this off if everybody was coddling me, asking me how I was, and reminding me it wasn't my fault. None of that, no matter how well intentioned it was, was going to help.

And none of it was true.

It was my fault, all of it, and I had every intention of fixing it. I was going to give them back Maddy, become Maddy. But in order for me to do that, I needed them to stop making me miss myself.

I jammed the key into the ignition, my entire body vibrating with so much anger that I could barely get my hands to move. After three tries and one silent plea for strength, I finally got the key to turn a notch, far enough to get the radio and heat going. I wasn't going to cry. I refused to cry. But my hands shook, and tears I hadn't let fall in days came pouring out. I cursed each one, tried to banish them all to the tightly locked box I held inside my mind.

This was a brand-new car. It smelled like leather and new carpet. Different make. Different model. The car I'd totaled was a pale blue Honda. This was a Ford Explorer. It was a different color—black—and there wasn't a lip gloss tube stuck to the floor or cleats shoved under the back-seat. There were no pictures of Alex taped to the glove box, no discarded bra stuffed under the floor mat. So how was it possible that no matter where I looked, all I saw was her?

I didn't want to do this. I couldn't. The simple task of putting the car in reverse, tapping the gas, and driving the same route I had to school for years suddenly seemed impossible. My hands shook, my knuckles going white as I grasped the steering wheel. My mind was racing along the street and I could feel every turn, every catch of the tire as I struggled to stay on the road. It was so real, so present, and yet only in my mind.

The tree I'd hit had been cut down, the cement curb replaced, or so Alex had said. The only remnant left from that night was a wooden cross with Ella's name . . . my name etched into it. And to get to school, to get anywhere, I'd have to drive by it.

I swore and let my head fall to the steering wheel. Maddy wouldn't be sitting here in the driveway frozen in panic. She would've driven away by now, swallowed down her fear and simply done it. She was that confident, that determined. And if I had any hope of truly becoming my sister, then I needed to be as well.

"Maddy," Mom called as she knocked on the window. I rolled it down. She reached for me, and I flinched. I didn't want to be soothed. I didn't deserve it.

"Why don't you let me drive you today? We'll get some breakfast on the way and then I'll drop you off later. Nobody expects you to—"

I shook my head and held my hand up for her to stop. That was where she was wrong. "Everybody expects me to," I fired back, remembering my last conversation with Maddy. Everybody expected something from her, wasn't that what she said? That it would be easier to be like me, to have nobody expect anything from you? "I expect myself to."

It took more effort than I ever would have imagined to turn the key that last notch. I heard the ignition catch, felt it waver as if it were in tune with me. I picked my head up and swiped at my tears. "I gotta go," I said as I put the car into gear.

There was no point in looking back as I pulled out of the driveway. I knew Mom would be standing there, watching, hoping that I'd let her help.

15

I was a senior and hadn't missed more than a week of school ever. I knew every hallway and how to make my way from the gym to the parking lot without having to pass by the office or cafeteria. I knew the exact number of steps it took to get from Josh's locker to mine and could navigate his combination as easily as my own. I knew the gym floor had been replaced last year and that there was a small hole above the mirror in the boys' locker room, one that looked directly into the girls' showers. There wasn't a thing about this school that should have surprised me, and yet, today, standing in the parking lot, staring up at the front doors, it seemed foreign.

I reached out, my hand falling short of the door handle. I felt like a freshman—not knowing who I'd meet or what I was walking into, hoping people would accept me, terrified that they wouldn't. But unlike that first day of school our freshman year, I didn't have my sister as a buffer. Today, I was truly on my own.

You can do this, I said to myself as I willed my hand to rise and demanded that my feet shuffle those few paces into the school. I had friends here. Maddy had friends here. And Maddy had Alex. I wasn't on my own. I just wasn't me.

Who knows what I expected to be waiting for me inside, but silence wasn't it. Quiet, hushed whispers followed me down the hall. My eyes caught the pitiful stares of two girls waiting outside the front office. I nodded and gave them a small wave. They quickly looked away, pretending to be interested in the notices hanging on the student info board. I think I preferred the hushed whispers to the pity I could feel pouring off them.

I picked up the pace and kept my eyes trained straight ahead as I tried to pretend they didn't exist. It was no use trying to insulate myself. No matter what way I looked, regardless of which hallway I turned down, they were still there—hundreds of eyes watching me, waiting for me to crack.

With my head down I shuffled along faster, but that didn't stop the sickening feeling from overtaking me. There was nowhere to hide. Ignoring my classmates didn't mean they weren't there, whispering about how I was doing.

I let my feet guide me, not once stopping to think where I was going. I rounded the corner and climbed two flights of stairs, my feet propelled by rote memory. I came to a stop in front of locker number 159 and reached for the combination lock. It wasn't until I had it open, until I saw Josh's most recent drawing taped to the inside of the door, that I realized where I was. My locker. Ella's locker.

The hall fell deadly silent, the muffled chatter that had followed me now gone. I dropped my backpack to the floor and searched my mind for something to say, some excuse . . . some justification for why I was here, for why I was standing in front of what everybody assumed was my dead sister's locker.

Alex broke the silence. I couldn't make out what he was saying: it was stifled and not intended for my ears. But I knew the inflection of his voice—the way it rasped when he was struggling to contain some emotion, how it ground deep when he was angry. Instinctively, I turned and sought him out. He'd help me—help Maddy—through this.

Josh was standing there, three lockers down, like he used to every morning before the accident. His dark, haunted eyes met mine, his gaze burrowing through me as if searching for the truth. I saw a flash of recognition, brief and full of forsaken hope before it faded away.

"Maddy?" Alex said.

I tore my eyes from Josh. I could handle the anger I'd seen in him at the burial and deal with the misplaced stares from my morbidly curious classmates, but what tore me apart was the agony I could feel radiating from Josh. I couldn't take his pain away, not without telling him I was Ella, not without crushing Alex and my parents, not without going back on my promise to Maddy . . . the one that traded my life for hers. Either way, somebody lost.

"Maddy?" Alex repeated. "What are you doing here?" he asked as he physically backed me away from the locker and kicked it shut with his foot. "Why are you going through Ella's locker?"

I shook my head, the physical motion jarring me back to the present. "Her stuff . . ." I said, not bothering to keep the emotion out of my voice. "Why is it still in there? Why has nobody cleaned it out?"

Alex looked past me to Josh as if somehow he had the answer. I watched the silent conversation play out between them, nothing more than an elaborate game of who was going to answer first. I'd never seen this before, never seen Josh hesitant to answer me, to talk to me. But then again, in his mind, in his reality, I was somebody completely different.

"Why?" I had to clear my throat, to swallow a mouthful of tears to get the words out. "Why is Ella's stuff still in there?" I asked again.

"I couldn't," Josh said as he turned around and buried his face in his own locker rather than look at me.

"Couldn't what?" I asked.

Josh ignored me, and I took a step toward him, wanting to demand an answer and soothe his grief at the same time. Alex stopped me, hooked his arm around my waist, and gently pulled me in to his chest.

"Your parents were going to do it. I offered to help. I

thought it'd be easier for everybody if I cleaned it out myself and brought her stuff home in a box. I figured you could go through it when you were ready," Alex told me.

"But—?" I asked when he paused.

"Josh wanted to do it himself. He promised me he'd have it done before you came back."

I caught the forgiveness in Alex's voice, knew he understood how hard this was for Josh. My guess was that that was why Alex had offered to clean out my locker in the first place—he wanted to spare Josh and my parents the pain of having to do it themselves.

I looked at my locker, then back to Josh. If it'd been him, if it was his locker that I'd been charged with clearing out, I'd have done the same thing: let everything he owned sit there undisturbed on some insane notion that he'd be back, that whatever had taken him from me was nothing more than an impossible nightmare I'd soon wake up from.

"I'll do it," I said as I yanked myself free of Alex's hold and emptied the contents of my bag onto the floor. I'd need to make two trips to my car to get everything out, but if it saved Josh from having to do it himself, I'd gladly be late for my first class.

The top shelf was easily cleared off, the textbooks stacked next to me on the floor. I'd turn those in to the office, or the teachers, or whoever was responsible for collecting textbooks, once I got everything else cleaned out. I went for the door and was carefully trying to peel the tape off the pictures when Josh exploded.

"Leave it!" he shouted. I'd never heard such rage in Josh's voice before or seen his body vibrate with such raw emotion. I stopped and looked at him, my hand still clutching the corner of a picture. "I. Said. Leave. It," he repeated.

I nodded and let it go, took two steps back to give him some space. He looked like he was about ready to lose it.

We'd accumulated quite a crowd of spectators. Every available body in the school—teachers and students alike—was there, waiting to see what I'd do. At this point I didn't care; they could grab some empty wall space and watch the show if that's what they wanted.

"Let it go," Alex whispered in my ear. "I'll talk to Josh and ask your parents to help clear Ella's locker out."

I nodded, knowing quite well that my parents wouldn't help Josh. They could barely enter my room, let alone go through my personal things. And from the looks of it, Josh had no intention of clearing out the remnants of my life either. He already had the textbooks stacked neatly back on the shelf and was smoothing out the crinkled photo on the door.

"I can help you," I said to Josh, hoping he wouldn't agree to my offer. I didn't want to spend time with him. I didn't want the constant reminder of who I once was, who I'd made the choice to never be again. What I wanted was for him to stop looking at me that way—with pain, anger, and hope rolled into one confused mess.

"I don't need your help," Josh said.

The anger I'd seen at the burial was back in place, and I sighed in relief. His anger I could deal with.

"Fine, if that's the way you want it," I said.

I turned to walk away, planning on leaving the discarded contents of my bag strewn across the hallway floor rather than spend one more second trapped in Josh's gaze. But his next, broken words stopped me, the truth he spoke echoing through my mind.

"That's not the way I want it. What I want is to see Ella again, but you can't help with that, can you?"

I tamped down the urge to respond, my good hand clutching Alex's so hard that I lost the feeling in my fingers. I couldn't do this here, not now. Not with Josh. Not with everybody, including Alex, watching.

"No. I can't," I said, not bothering to turn around and look my best friend in the eyes as I confirmed his worst nightmare. "She's gone, and I can't change that."

16

Alex was in my first period class. I didn't know if I was relieved or irritated about that. He'd remind people not to stare and make sure nobody said anything to me. But that also meant I had to play along, continue to be Maddy when what I truly wanted was five minutes alone to clear my head and regroup.

Hoping to avoid as many people as possible, I went in through the back door. Didn't work. Everybody's eyes, including Mr. Peterson's, swung in my direction.

Mr. Peterson smiled, the first genuine smile I'd seen this morning. "It's good to see you, Madison."

I managed a weak thank-you and let go of Alex's hand so I could take a seat in the corner. Mr. Peterson wasn't one of my teachers. He taught American Lit, not AP English like I was in, or even Honors English. This was general, run-of-the-mill American Lit.

The seat next to me was already taken, and I gave the kid occupying it credit. He didn't raise his head when I sat down. He ignored me and kept studying the etchings on his desk. I didn't know his name. I'd seen him wandering the halls and in the parking lot, but that was it.

"There's a seat in the front row," Alex said as he dropped his bag to the floor and waited for the kid to move.

The kid glanced up at Alex and then to me as if waiting for approval. "What's your name?" I asked.

Alex looked curious as to why I suddenly cared who this kid was. I didn't care so much as I was jealous. Nobody knew him. Nobody bothered with him. He was a lot like me before I decided to become Maddy.

"Ryan," he said.

"It's fine, Alex. I'm fine. Ryan can stay," I said.

I didn't hear what Alex mumbled under his breath as he walked away and took a seat in the front row next to Jenna. But to be honest, I wasn't paying much attention. I was more interested in fading into the background like the boy sitting next to me.

I shuffled through my bag and pulled out a notebook labeled *Lit*. Save for a few versions of Alex's name covering the first pages, it was completely empty, not a single note on any page. Grumbling, I looked over at Ryan's desk. He didn't have a pen out, never mind a notebook.

"This is American Lit, right?" I said, trying to confirm what I already knew.

Ryan raised his head and stared at me, no pity, no curiosity, absolutely nothing in his eyes. "Yeah, why?"

I shrugged, not knowing how to respond. Because it was three months into school and I already had a binder full of notes for AP English. Because I'd read four books, dissected each one, and written a seven-page essay on each. Because I had no idea what was going on in this class, and from the lack of notes Maddy had, it appeared she didn't either.

Someone kicked my shoe, and I turned to my right. I remembered her. She was the girl from the party, the one sitting on the couch crying. I stared at her for a moment, finally recognizing who she was. Without the noise of the party and the makeup streaming down her face, I actually recognized her. Molly.

She used to be one of Maddy's friends. Something happened to her last year, though, something to do with a field hockey game and testing positive for drugs. I'd learned some of the details from listening to Maddy. Molly had lost her spot on the field hockey team and the scholarship she was nearly guaranteed to get from Northwestern. On top of that, the incident took her from being more popular than Maddy to being barely one rung above me on the social ladder. She still sat with Maddy's group at lunch and was invited to the same parties, but to say she operated on the fringe of their circle was being generous at best.

"Hey, Molly—" I started to say something more, but she waved me off and tilted her head toward the front of the class.

I had a brief moment of panic, wondering if Mr. Peterson was angry with me for talking in class. But Mr. Peterson wasn't trying to get my attention, Alex was. He tossed his hands out in a what-are-you-doing gesture, then motioned to Ryan. He didn't need words to convey his message; I got it loud and clear. In Maddy's world, Alex took center stage. Whatever he wanted, whatever he needed, Maddy gave it to him. If I wanted to pull this off, then I needed to stop talking to the nameless kids in the back of the room and start focusing on him.

Nodding my apology, I took up Ryan's favorite pastime and started reading the etchings on the desk. I'd finished counting the number of times the f-word could be used as a descriptor and was hazarding a guess at whose initials were in the heart when a piece of paper covered my desk.

"Try your best," Mr. Peterson whispered. "I won't grade it."

I wrote my name and date on the paper. I missed nearly a month of school, and on my first day back, I had to take a test.

The book's title was in bold letters across the top, two questions posed in italics below. *East of Eden.* I read it freshman year; it was on the summer reading list for those of us who had tested into the advanced track. Had I known there was a test today, I would've dug it out and reread a few chapters so I'd have quotes to support my answers.

I glanced at the first question and started writing my answer, worrying that I would forget something important. I remembered enough of the book to formulate a decent response. It wouldn't be an A, but it wouldn't be a C either.

Mr. Peterson had given us nearly the entire fifty minutes of class time to take the test, and according to the clock on the wall, I had twelve minutes left. I looked over my answers twice before I put my pen down. Writing those two responses had felt great, like a little part of the old me was safe to come out. An old part of me that was still useful.

I took a quick peek at Ryan's test. He had three sentences down for the first answer and was struggling his way through the first paragraph of the second. A quick look at Molly's proved that she was no better off. There was less than ten minutes left of class, and she hadn't even started on the second question. I'd been to one class, had spent less than an hour in school as Maddy, and already I'd screwed up. I'd *read the book* for American Lit and actually *answered* the questions.

Frustrated, I balled up my test and pushed it aside. That sound, the crumpling of paper in my hand, echoed through the room, every head swinging in my direction. Alex, Jenna, Molly, even Ryan stared at me.

"I can't do this," I said, and stood up.

"Nobody expects your best work on your first day

back." Mr. Peterson approached me, his eyes wary, his tone a little too gentle to be comforting. He stopped a few feet from me, his attention turning to the balled-up test on my desk. When I made no motion to pick it up myself, he reached for it, smoothed it out between his hands, and began to read.

His lips moved silently with the words, and he flipped the paper over as the arrow I'd drawn on the bottom of the page indicated him to do. I knew what he was doing, knew the instant he turned it over for a second read that he was trying to figure out how Maddy had pulled this off. How some girl, fresh out of the hospital and still stricken with grief—the same girl who'd barely managed to pull a C in his class—had written this.

His eyes widened. A look of pure astonishment crossed his face, and I stumbled backward, knocking my chair over. Alex stood up, motioning to Jenna to stay seated when she started to follow him.

"Maddy?" Mr. Peterson laid his hand on my arm, tried to drag my attention back to him. "Maddy, this is good."

"I know," I whispered as I scrambled toward the door. "That's the problem. It's too good."

I heard Alex behind me, saying something about taking care of it. I didn't wait for him to catch up. I ran as fast as I could down the hall to the one place I knew Alex wouldn't follow me, the one place in this entire building I knew of that had doors with locks.

17

The bathroom was completely empty. *My only* company was the sound of the old radiator struggling to pump heat. I walked to the last stall and locked myself in. Alex was at the main door, knocking and calling out my name. I half-expected him to come in. Part of me wanted him to so I could wrap myself in his arms and selfishly believe it when he promised me it'd be okay.

I chased away my thoughts of Maddy, of the accident, of Josh. My mother's tears, the whispers that threatened to suffocate me, and the burrowing eyes of the entire school. I needed them gone.

My mind cleared slowly and the dingy tiles of the bathroom floor blurred together in a clutter of gray. I was perfectly content to sit there forever, but the bell rang, the shrill sound filtering in, growing louder as the door opened and closed in rapid sequence. Not wanting to be noticed, I pulled my feet up onto the seat and stayed silent.

I heard bits and pieces of the gossip I'd missed over the past few weeks. Jenna was vying for the title of Snow Ball queen, but I figured that. She may have been Maddy's best friend, but I'd caught the spark of jealousy hidden behind those blue eyes.

"I gotta say, when it comes to campaigning though, Jenna's got one amazing platform. I mean, what guy *wouldn't* vote for her—"

I don't know which of Maddy's idiotic friends came out with that line, but she was absolutely right about Jenna using her assets to get ahead. As far as I could tell, her personality was about as deadly as the plague, so using her figure was probably her best option for gaining votes.

"She won't win. Alex will make sure of that. Plus, Maddy's got the pity vote. That's gotta count for something."

I cringed at her words, remembering a conversation I'd overheard last month. Maddy had been in the bathroom at home, her phone on speaker so she could talk and put her makeup on at the same time. She and Alex were strategizing, going over who they thought would vote for who. At last check, Maddy and Jenna were tied. I didn't hear Alex's plan to fix that—whatever he was saying was garbled by the sound of running water. All I heard was Maddy arguing with him, something about her last plan having gone horribly wrong.

I let it go, didn't bother to stay and listen to what that

meant. Maddy had a way of being theatrical and was probably flying off the handle about something as unimportant as a chipped nail.

I shook off the memory and stopped listening to the girls in the bathroom, more concerned about what I was going to do if Maddy . . . if *I* actually won the title of Snow Ball queen. That would mean wearing a dress and heels, having my hair and nails done, dancing with Alex, and a crapload of smiling and kissing up to people I didn't like. None of which I had any desire to do. All of which Maddy would have done without a second thought.

Someone tried to yank open the stall door, then knocked and bent down to peer underneath. I inched farther back on the seat and tried to make myself invisible, but she saw me anyway—it's not like there was a huge amount of space for hiding in a three-by-three-foot cage. Molly's face came into view, and I waved my hands frantically at her. I wordlessly begged her not to say anything, not to reveal to the few girls still in the bathroom that I was camped out in the last stall, hiding.

She nodded, her small, sad smile reminding me that she'd been here herself not long ago.

"You okay?" she mouthed.

"Yes," I whispered back.

"The door is broken again," she said to some random girls as she straightened up. "Go use the one next to it."

The bathroom cleared, and the noise in the hall quieted down. The next class had started, the entire school going on with their day without me. Slowly I dropped my feet to the floor and opened the stall door. I half-expected somebody to be waiting for me. Maybe Molly. Maybe Jenna. But the bathroom was empty, not even the radiator was making noise anymore.

A long, scratched-up mirror covered the entire wall, making it impossible not to catch a glimpse of myself. I looked hollow and pathetic. Maddy wouldn't look like this. Maddy wouldn't hide in a bathroom stall afraid of what people were thinking or saying about her. She'd listen, then twist their words so that she came out on top. I'd seen her do it enough times. I'd even ended up on the twisted side myself more than once.

I fixed my hair, did what I'd seen Maddy do a thousand times—flipped my head upside down and shook it. I didn't stop until my world spun, which, incidentally, was three shakes in. One last look in the mirror and I opened the door.

18

Alex pushed off from the wall across from the bathroom when he saw me come out. He must have been standing there waiting for me for at least ten minutes. He had my backpack in one hand, his cell phone in the other. He looked up at me briefly, then back to his phone to finish whatever he was texting.

"Hey," I said as I took my backpack from his outstretched hand.

I don't know what I expected. Perhaps that he'd hold me or offer to skip his next class and sit with me. Maybe make an attempt to talk me down off the crazy ledge I was teetering on, but what I got was a confusing glare and a nod.

"I saw Molly come out of the bathroom before you," Alex said as he shoved his phone into his pocket. "She looked . . . I don't know, better."

I wasn't aware she looked like crap to begin with. "Better than what?"

"Better than she has since she came back. You say something to her?"

I winced, unable to hide the surprise in my face. I'd said hi to her in class and silently begged her not to tell the other girls in the bathroom that I was crouched up on a toilet hiding out, but that was it. Nothing earth-shattering, nothing remotely helpful or sympathetic.

"No, I didn't say anything to her, but why would it matter if I did?"

"We talked about this at the party, Maddy. It's safer if we keep her on the outside."

Alex took a step forward, his body suddenly within inches of mine. I could smell his cologne, see the smooth lines of his jaw and the tiny spot he'd missed when shaving this morning. "You have to trust me on this. You need to keep your distance from her, at least until things settle down and you're feeling more like yourself."

The pain in his voice stabbed at my heart and I shook my head. There was a fear behind his words, a fear that I would change my mind and reveal a secret I didn't even know. My reply was easy, I wouldn't tell Molly anything— not because I was trying to protect him or my sister, but because I had no clue what he was talking about.

"I wasn't planning on telling Molly anything," I said.

I felt his relief and offered him my hand. He took it and laced his fingers through mine. "What happened with Molly is in the past, Maddy, and it needs to stay there."

Every part of me was begging to ask him what he was talking about. I searched his expression for a clue as to what was going on between Alex and Maddy, and what Molly had to do with it. I got nothing.

I tried to think of a time when something seemed off between them. I remembered the muffled conversation in the bathroom the week before Maddy died—the one about some plan of Maddy's going wrong—and I remembered the tears streaming down Maddy's face at the party. But other than that, everything between Maddy and Alex had seemed fine. Perfect, actually.

Alex took my silence for indecision and reached out to tuck a stray lock of hair behind my ear. "I made sure everything went away. Made certain you got to be co-captain of the field hockey team, prom queen in junior year, the girl everybody wants to be, didn't I?"

I nodded because agreeing with him seemed like the logical thing to do.

"Seven more months and we're out of here. We can start over and forget everything that happened. I can keep things together for you until then, but you've gotta stop trying to make amends with Molly and remember who *you* are, how you got here, and what you've been willing to do to make sure nobody, including Molly, stands in your way."

Whatever this was, whatever lie my sister and Alex were covering up, I hadn't agreed to it. I thought I could put on her clothes, sit in her classes, talk to her friends, and make everybody so happy she was alive that they'd overlook tiny mistakes I made here and there. But this was different. Complicated. Too complicated.

I stared at Alex, unable to speak, unable to wipe the look of sheer confusion from my face. I would have been more than happy to hand the crown of popularity over to Jenna and sink into the background. But what I wanted didn't matter. The most important thing was keeping Maddy's life intact, every piece of it, including this.

Alex caught the frustration on my face, his tone purposefully gentling as he pulled out his phone and started to dial my dad's number. "Maybe your parents were right. Maybe it was too soon for you to come back to school. Maybe you should go and talk to the therapist with your parents, give yourself some more time before—"

"I don't need to talk to anybody." I reached for the phone and hit the Off button before the call connected to my father's office. "I'm fine, Alex, honest. People are acting weird around me, and it makes me . . . I don't know, edgy." The words tumbled out as I desperately tried to bluff my way through the rest of the conversation. Until I figured out what I'd walked into, I needed to keep my cards close. Watch more and say less.

"Probably because *you're* acting weird around *them*," he said. The concern and confusion that had dampened his features for the past month were suddenly gone, the confident Alex I was used to seeing with Maddy back in place.

"Plus, edgy is good. That's what they're used to. It's freaking out in class and hiding in the bathroom that is going to get you in trouble."

"I know," I said, trying to sound convincing.

"Molly is where she is today because she didn't have the strength that you do. And, she didn't have me. There are plenty of people here willing to take your place. One wrong move and you'll be exactly where she is now—at the bottom, staring up at where you *used* to be. I can help you, cover for you and keep you safe, make sure that doesn't happen, but you gotta let me. You gotta stop shutting me out and talk to me *before* you lose it."

I nodded. He wasn't telling me anything I didn't already know.

"Listen, Maddy. You can fall apart at home with me if you have to, but I need you to hold it together while we're here. If you can't do that, then let me take you home, because trust me, it's not worth undoing everything we've worked so hard to get."

"I'm fine," I said again as I hitched my backpack farther up on my shoulder. A chill raced along my spine as I considered my limited options—play the popular sister or go home. The choice was easy. For the foreseeable future, I'd keep my mouth shut, not talk to anybody but Alex, and, if I was smart, start paying better attention to the conversations going on around me. Clearly I'd missed something . . . a lot of things. And if I was going to survive this mess, I needed to learn about Maddy's past, fast.

Until that epiphany hit, I'd focus on the small stuff. I'd avoid passing any American Lit tests by more than the bare minimum. I'd feign interest in choosing the color scheme for the Snow Ball, fake interest when Jenna went on about her dress, and come up with something catty to say about the ten pounds her sister had gained. I'd start treating everybody else the way I was used to Maddy treating me—with indifference.

"You have study hall next," he reminded me.

"Umm hmm." I knew Maddy's schedule, made sure I had it memorized before I set foot in school.

"Try to say something nice to Jenna. She's still bent out of shape that you have been avoiding her. But don't mention her parents losing the house or her brother having to drop out of college and work at their uncle's garage. She doesn't want anybody to know, especially you. If she finds out I told you, she'll never forgive me . . . or you."

They could find another house, but Jenna's brother—he was the pride and joy of the family. He'd graduated when we were freshmen and he'd gotten a scholarship to Notre Dame, the same school his father and grandfather graduated from. I'd met him once when he came to pick up Jenna at our house. He had seemed nice enough . . . nice enough that I actually felt bad for him.

"Ask her about what happened between her and Keith while you were out of school," Alex added, and I stopped thinking about Jenna's brother stocking parts at the garage to help with bills and focused on Alex's words.

"That will keep her talking for a while so you don't have to."

Alex spun me around and headed me in the opposite direction from him, a silent message to not screw up barely hidden in his voice: "I know it sucks, Maddy, but remember, the sooner things get back to normal, the better off we'll both be."

19

I walked in the direction Alex had nudged me toward. I wasn't anxious to hear Jenna talk about herself, but standing there in the hall staring wide-eyed at Alex was not going to help. Normal. That was what I was striving for. Problem was, I had no idea what Maddy's version of normal was.

Mine was sitting in my room drawing or arguing with Josh over whether or not banana peppers and chicken was a good combination of pizza toppings. My normal was constant. The people around me were predictable. I could tell you that Josh had a poppy seed bagel with veggie cream cheese every morning for breakfast. I could tell you that he never filled his tank past the quarter mark and always went to the 7-Eleven on Reservoir Avenue because it was the only one that had watermelon Slurpees. He'd bring two brand-new mechanical pencils to every test, same make, same brand. One for me, one for him.

But Maddy's friends . . . Alex . . . there was nothing predictable or consistent about them.

I didn't have a clue what I was supposed to do. I'd never had a study hall in my life. I always filled those empty spots with an open studio or an advanced class. Plus, I had nothing to study. In fact, if I wanted to play the part of Maddy, then I needed to dumb myself down, not get a jump start on tomorrow's homework.

The halls were pretty much empty. A couple of girls were heading toward the bathroom and a few more were digging forgotten books or homework assignments out of their lockers. The rest of the students were in their classes. Having nowhere in particular to go, I slowed my pace. It was nice to be alone, to have a second of peace to reorient myself.

I had forty-five minutes until my next real class started, and I thought I'd use it to sift through the contents of Maddy's locker. I'd already gone through her desk, bureau, and closet. None of those revealed anything out of the ordinary, except perhaps the box of condoms I found shoved down in the toe of one of her boots this morning.

I don't know where the urge to count them came from, but I did. Box of twelve, seven left. That only confirmed my suspicion that Alex wasn't kidding when he joked that

I'd be ready soon. Yeah, no clue how I was going to handle that one.

I slowed nearly to a stop when I heard Jenna's voice. She couldn't see me; there was a bank of lockers blocking her view, but I doubted seeing me would've stopped her. I carefully eased my way forward until she came into full view. I intended to do as Alex had instructed and pretend to be interested in what Jenna had to say. I mean, how hard could it be? All I had to do was smile and nod every once in a while.

I counted the lockers three times to make sure I wasn't mistaken, then searched the numbers for further confirmation: that was Maddy's locker Jenna was standing in front of.

But it was my name—Ella—mingled into Jenna's conversation that had my ears trained on her words. I shrank into the lockers out of Jenna's view and let the cold metal support me as I stood there and listened.

"Alex is angry that we didn't have this done before she got here this morning," Jenna was saying.

She had a roll of crepe paper in one hand, a giant poster board in the other. She tore off a chunk of streamer paper and waved at the girl next to her to hurry up and give her some tape. "If he wanted her locker decorated with this welcome-back crap, then he should've done it himself. Like the one in the locker room isn't enough."

The girl laughed as she dug some sort of homemade sign out of her backpack. I couldn't read the names on it from where I was hiding, but there were a lot. She tacked it to the front of my locker and offered Jenna a pen. Jenna shook her head and shoved the pen away.

"I don't know why he's mad. It's not like anybody knew she'd be here today," the girl said.

Jenna nodded, playing along. Leave it to her to play innocent. She knew I was coming back today. I was sitting next to Alex on my bed last night when he called her and told her to tell our "friends" not to ask me any questions about the accident or Ella. Apparently, she'd conveniently forgotten to pass that message on.

"Did you see her at Ella's locker this morning?" I still couldn't place who that girl was—probably an underclassman or one of the JV field hockey players that Jenna had promised a varsity spot to. "She lost it on that weird boy her sister used to always hang out with. I kind of feel bad for her. It's got to be hard facing him."

Josh wasn't weird; he was the most genuine person I knew. And I wouldn't qualify me trying to clear out my *own* locker as losing it. I'd call it being considerate of Josh's feelings.

Jenna nodded and stepped back to admire her work. Maddy's entire locker was covered with streamers and well wishes scribbled on Post-it notes. "Yeah, well, what did you expect? You kill your sister in a car accident, you're bound to be a little messed up."

There it was, that snap of brutal honesty that I'd always associated with Jenna.

I remembered asking my sister about her when we were freshmen. It was toward the end of the year. Jenna had become a constant fixture in my sister's life and the bane of my existence. I didn't get what my sister saw in her, and why she chose to surround herself with such mean people.

"She's not as bad as you think. I mean, you don't even know her," Maddy said as she flicked through the TV channels. Mom had grounded us for arguing over whose turn it was to empty the dishwasher. We'd been arguing about everything back then, from who didn't put the cap back on the milk to who was smarter. Our punishment was a weekend at home with nobody to talk to but each other.

I rolled my eyes. I didn't need to know Jenna. I'd watched her flip off some random girl at school that day, for looking at whatever boy she had marked as her own, and heard her tear an exchange student a new one in the cafeteria the day before for accidentally sitting down in her seat.

"She's mean, Maddy. No matter how you slice it, that girl is mean."

"You would be too if you had her life."

I highly doubted that, but whatever, I'd bite. "Why? What possible excuse are you going to make for her?"

"She went to the same elementary and middle school as Alex," Maddy began. "She has lived next door to him since first grade, and their parents are good friends."

I found that interesting, or at least it made sense as to

why Maddy had started hanging out with her to begin with—they had Alex in common.

"Her mom is insanely neurotic about appearances and her dad is never around. He works overseas or something, barely even calls when he's traveling."

I shrugged. Josh's dad was a pilot and was gone for days at a time, but Josh wasn't a jerk because of it. "So?"

"Everything has to be perfect in their world. Her room, her hair, her grades, everything. I'm over there nearly every day and the only things I have ever heard her parents say to her are 'Why can't you be as smart as your brother?' and 'Why can't you be as pretty as your sister?' Never once have I heard them say 'Good job' or 'It's okay, we love you the way you are.' Not once. But you know what Alex says?"

I shook my head. Alex never said much of anything to me, with the exception of "Hey" whenever he came to pick up Maddy. So no, I had no idea what his take on Jenna was. And to be honest, I don't think I actually cared.

"Alex says it's a show. That they borrowed money from his parents last week to cover their mortgage."

"She told you this?" I asked, amazed that Jenna would show any vulnerability to my sister.

"No, Alex did, but he made me swear not to tell anyone, so you can't either."

Who was I going to tell? Josh? I doubted he cared about Jenna's personal life any more than I did, which was already very little. "So you're saying it's okay for somebody to be mean because they have crappy parents?"

Maddy sighed and tossed the TV remote aside. She was irritated, as if trying to explain her best friend's motives to me was a chore. "No, Ella, I'm saying her life sucks. Dad doesn't care whether I make the varsity team this year or if you end up valedictorian. And Mom doesn't swallow a handful of pills just so she can get out of bed and put her makeup on each morning. Jenna's the way she is because *not* being the best at everything isn't an option for her. It's the only way to get her parents' attention, the only time her father ever acknowledges her existence."

I didn't buy that excuse three years ago when Maddy first fed it to me, and I wasn't buying it now. Sure, maybe Jenna became self-centered, competitive, and mean to earn her father's attention, but somewhere along the line it stopped being about her parents' approval and became all about her.

"She's your best friend," the girl said to Jenna as she smoothed out the wrinkles in the center of the poster. "Don't you think you should talk to her? I mean, maybe see if you can help?"

I smiled at her words. I may not have known who she was, but the way she quietly tried to defend me made me feel better and more at ease with some of my sister's friends.

"Alex will make sure she's okay," Jenna replied as she adjusted one of the streamers so it didn't cover the poster.

"And, according to him, she's steps away from a total breakdown. I'm supposed to give her some space and not bother her too much."

She was right, I'd give her that. Since I'd come home from the hospital, I'd refused to leave the house, refused to see anyone but my parents and Alex. He'd been given depressed-Maddy duty. Jenna had called a million times the first few days, but I'd either let her calls go to voice mail or had Alex talk to her. The longer I refused to answer, the fewer calls came. Or so I thought at first. Then I realized the calls had kept coming, but they were now going to Alex's phone and not Maddy's.

"Wait. What? You've been talking to Alex? We asked him how she was doing, but he won't tell any of us a thing. He keeps saying she's fine. How did you get him to talk to you?"

"I'm her best friend, remember?" Jenna's sarcasm had me wanting to reach through time and space to grab my sister and shake her. Maddy could have done better than this, she'd deserved a better friend than Jenna. "Plus, I have known Alex since first grade. I probably know him better than Maddy does. Of course he talks to me. About everything," Jenna added.

I didn't know Alex well, but I'd stake my life on the fact that he didn't tell Jenna much of anything . . . not when it involved Maddy, anyway. He kept her secrets safe, protected her with a fierceness that almost made me jealous.

I watched as Jenna unrolled a giant poster, one that, from the looks of it, had been professionally printed. She had matching tape, too—the exact same shade as the pink block lettering she'd used to spell out her name.

"You sure that's the best place for that?"

"Hallways are fair game," Jenna said as she reached up and put her Snow Ball queen poster dead center above Maddy's locker. "The only place we're prohibited from soliciting votes is in the field house and the locker rooms, although—"

"I think you're wasting your time. Maddy's gonna get so many pity votes that you won't be able to compete. I mean, she may look like crap, but who wouldn't vote for her after what happened?"

"You, for starters," Jenna said. I heard the calm threat in her voice. Somehow she'd figure out who would vote for her and who wouldn't. For that girl, casting a vote for Maddy would be equal to social suicide.

"Besides," Jenna continued, "Maddy can't be the Snow Ball queen if she's not going to the dance. Alex will only coddle her for so long, then eventually he's gonna get tired of tiptoeing around her."

My sister's image, the one she had meticulously crafted, was being torn apart while I stood here hiding. I knew what Maddy would do. I knew without a doubt that she'd walk down that hall and call Jenna out. They'd argue and threaten each other with useless pieces of gossip, then come four o'clock, it'd be over. Whatever nasty words had passed between them would be forgotten and someone else's misfortune would take the spotlight.

Not me. I'd quietly walk away without ever letting Jenna know I'd heard every backstabbing word that came out of her mouth. I'd plot and plan, sit at home and stew, rehash everything Jenna Fredricks had said about me, then I'd let it go. I'd pick up my sketchbook and lose myself in the drawing of a dead tree while I tried to forget that Jenna even existed.

20

I turned back the way I'd come, my head down, my mind completely focused on the texture and shade of the dead tree I was already sketching in my mind. No colored pencils for this picture. There was going to be nothing but black charcoal intermingled with gray smudges.

I felt someone's hands reach out and brush my arm in an attempt to stop me before I plowed her over. It didn't work, and I found myself staring up at Molly, my books scattered everywhere.

"Sorry," I mumbled, and quickly turned to look over my shoulder.

Molly shrugged and looked past me toward Maddy's locker. I turned and followed her gaze, hoping to God Jenna wasn't still standing there. The last thing I needed was an audience, an audience that Alex had insisted I play nice with.

"You okay?" she asked, her eyes still trained on Maddy's locker.

"Yeah. I guess so." I didn't know whether she was referring to Jenna's comments, the bathroom episode, or the accident in general. Probably a combination of all three. I quickly gathered my books and shoved them into my bag. "Were you . . . uh . . . listening to them?"

She nodded, and held out her hand to help me up. I took it, grateful that at least one of my sister's friends didn't seem to be completely self-absorbed.

Molly stood there staring at me, her lips parting as if she was debating whether or not to tell me something.

"What?" I said, wanting her to come out with it. I was tired of trying to piece things together, guessing my way through Maddy's life. For once, I needed someone to tell me how it was.

"Nothing."

I sighed and walked away, disgusted with myself for foolishly hoping one of Maddy's friends could be honest.

"I ran into Jenna last weekend at the game." The words spilled out of Molly's mouth as if she wanted to say everything before she had a chance to change her mind. "They were standing outside by the field house. She didn't see me there."

I turned around to face her, fighting my curiosity to ask exactly who "they" were. I doubted it was Alex. He'd shown up at my house twenty minutes after the game ended, still wearing his grungy soccer cleats and grass-covered shorts. He smelled, too, like sweat and dirt.

"She was talking to Eva."

The blank look on my face must have clued her in. "You know, the freshman? Crappy midfielder on the JV field hockey team? Idiot who actually thinks that hanging with Jenna will somehow get her a spot on the varsity team?" She tilted her head and stared at me when I didn't respond. "You know, the one who was at your locker with Jenna?"

I nodded, grateful to finally have a name to put with the voice. Then I lied: "I know who she is. What about her?"

"She and Jenna were talking about Alex and how Jenna thinks he's wasting his time with you."

I shrugged. "So?"

"She's after more than Alex, you know. Jenna wants the Snow Ball crown and since you haven't played in almost a month, she is trying to get Coach to replace you as co-captain of the field hockey team. Jenna pretty much promised it to Eva. I felt like I should say something because—"

"My life already sucks?" I finished for her.

"Well, yeah. I didn't want to see it get worse. I mean, I've been there. I know what it's like."

Been there? According to Alex, she was *still* there.

I watched her eyes glaze over and could tell she was remembering something that neither time nor distance could make disappear. I knew because it happened to me every day. Every hour. Every minute.

"That night at the party, you were crying," I said. "Why?"

A brief flash of confusion crossed Molly's face at my question, her eyes quickly softening. I knew in that instant what the look meant, the mistake I had made. Maddy would know why she was crying. She would have made it her business to know.

"You don't remember?" Molly asked.

I shuffled my feet as I tried uselessly to come up with something to say, an excuse or a lie that would keep everything intact. But I came up empty. I could do nothing but stare blankly at her.

"I get it," Molly said. "I had a hard time remembering ever taking any drugs. But then again, everybody said it was because I didn't want to remember, that I was denying it to save myself. At least you have the accident to blame for not remembering stuff."

My hand automatically went to my head, to the scar where my stitches once were. I rubbed it, thinking how much easier it would be if what she said were true, if in fact my mind had stayed as empty as it was when I first woke up, and I didn't know a thing.

I remembered the rumor that had circulated about Molly last year. People said she'd been taking pills for months, that that was why she was so good on the field, why she had an insane amount of energy. When she denied it, carrying on about the drug test results being wrong or about being set up, people said she was crazy and that she was paranoid and delusional. I guess she was. She used to sit in the cafeteria and zone out, not talk to anybody. One time I saw Alex try to talk to her, and she'd lashed out at him, jumping up from her seat and staring at him like he was a psycho. He'd done nothing but gently shake her arm to get her attention, and she freaked, accused him of somehow being involved.

The same thing happened the next weekend at the state championship. She went to watch. The coach let her sit on the bench, but she wasn't allowed to wear her uniform or even her practice shirt. She stared off into space as the game was played around her, never once acknowledging the players sitting next to her. They lost; with Cranston High's best player benched, they didn't stand a chance.

Molly wasn't at school that next week. None of us knew where she went, but we had our assumptions. Six weeks later she showed up, quiet and withdrawn. Everyone avoided her. My sister, Jenna, Alex—they let her sit at their table in the cafeteria, but they stopped including her in their conversations, stopped caring enough to ask what she thought. Maddy claimed that was the way Molly wanted it, that whenever anybody tried to talk to her she'd tell them to go away and leave her alone. I refused to believe that. My guess was that they didn't know what to say to her, how to make things go back to normal, so it was easier for Maddy and the rest of them to shut her out.

"I won't tell anybody that things are still hazy for you if that's what you're worried about," Molly said. "I get what it's like not knowing exactly what happened, trying to solve a puzzle when you're not even sure what the pieces are."

I wasn't worried about figuring things out. With the exception of Alex, I think everybody already assumed I was one step away from losing it.

"Thanks," I said, and waited to see if she would tell me about the party. Tell me why she was crying. Why Maddy was sitting alone in the backyard. Why Jenna was in a particularly nasty mood. But she said nothing, let the awkward silence between us grow to a suffocating level.

Searching for something to say and coming up empty, I did the one thing I could. I started to walk away.

"You asked me to go to that party, said it wasn't fair what had happened to me and that these were my friends and you were going to make it right."

I stopped dead in my tracks and turned around.

"Alex whispered something to you when I walked in. I don't know what it was, but he seemed pissed. You had a fight later that night, but I don't know what it was about. Maybe about me being there," she said as she took a step in my direction.

I didn't know what the fight had been about, but rather than admit that, I asked again, "Why were *you* crying? What happened?"

"Jenna. She was there being her usual self."

Molly didn't need to explain that. I'd been on the receiving end of Jenna's nasty comments for years. I was well aware that she had probably taken Molly's tears and used them as a way to gain the upper hand, remind her that she was different. Damaged. Useless.

"Jenna's a self-serving wannabe. I don't get why you—" I paused for a second to correct myself. "I don't get why we hang out with her."

"I don't anymore. You do."

I shrugged, not knowing what to say. I guessed, at the end of the day, I would classify Jenna as my sister's best friend. I'd gladly go the next seven months, the next seven years, my entire life as Maddy, but there was no way I was putting up with Jenna in the process. "Yeah . . . well, I have a feeling that's gonna change."

Molly smirked, no doubt understanding exactly what I meant. "I figured that much at the party."

I cocked my head, pretended I was searching my mind for a lost piece of information. "I . . . uhh . . ."

The amusement faded from Molly's eyes, a pain I was familiar with replacing it. "You heard her prodding me and lost it, said you were done with her treating me that way. Done pretending that none of this was your fault."

I didn't dare ask what "this" referred to. Besides, the look on Molly's face told me she wouldn't know the answer anyway, that she was as confused, as curious as me about what Maddy had been so upset about. Unfortunately, I didn't have the answer either.

"I'm sorry. There is a lot of stuff from that night I still can't remember."

"Alex heard you yelling at Jenna and came in," Molly said. "He grabbed you and told you to be quiet before you ruined everything. You screamed at him to let you go, to leave you alone. I went to help you, but he told me to stay out of it, that you were drunk and that he'd take care of it."

"I wasn't drunk." That was the one thing I was certain about. I'd seen Maddy drunk plenty of times, stumbling and giddy as I handed her ibuprofen and Gatorade at two in the morning, then lied to my parents about her having cramps the next day when she could barely move. That night, Maddy wasn't drunk. She was upset, maybe a little bit scared, but not drunk.

Plus, I had the hospital's blood test to prove it.

"I know you weren't drunk, but to Alex—"

"A drunk, rambling Maddy is easier to explain than the truth." I finished the thought for her.

She tossed her hands out in agreement, and for a moment, I remembered that she knew these people, these so-called friends better than I did. Probably better than Maddy did. "You think if I ignore them, if I give it a little bit of time, things will go back to normal?" I asked.

"Umm, no."

That was okay. After talking to Molly and seeing what my sister and her friends were capable of, I wasn't sure Maddy's normal was what I wanted.

21

*I eased open the door to the school's back stair-*case. Hardly anybody used it. It was out of the way, the third-floor entrance to it tucked between the art room and the janitor's closet. Most of the school preferred to use the main stairwell, whose wide steps dumped you within feet of the cafeteria, the front office, or the exit to the student parking lot. This narrow back staircase dumped you no-where but into the dark corners of each floor.

It was quiet, the echo of my own thoughts keeping me company, and that was what I wanted—an out-of-the-way space to think and regroup.

There was a large window midway up the stairs with a ledge big enough to sit on. There was fifteen minutes left of study hall and walking in this late would draw more attention to myself. Attention I didn't want or need. Not yet anyway.

I loved it here: the cold cinder blocks at my back, the heat vent below roasting my feet. I spent hours each week in this very spot, with my sketchpad, watching the world outside, trying to replicate in my drawings every movement, every dropped leaf, every parked car.

I reached down and grabbed a notebook out of Maddy's bag. It was lined, so I flipped to the only blank space I could find—the back cover—and dug around in the bag again until I found a pencil. It was nothing but a standard number 2 pencil, but it would do.

Lost in my drawing, I startled when the bell rang. The few people who used this staircase were making their way through the doors. I ignored them, my focus on the notebook in front of me and the janitor emptying trash into the Dumpster outside. If he would stay still for more than half a second, I'd get his expression down right. But he kept moving, picking up stray bits of paper that had blown free of the container.

The halls went quiet. My next class had started—Physics, I think. It was Basic Physics, not Honors. I could miss two months of that class and still come out with a B. Missing one more day wasn't gonna kill me. I had lunch, four more classes, two hours of field hockey practice to watch—a sport I didn't know how to play—and a crapload of homework to make up, and yet I couldn't get myself to move from that spot.

I tried to hold it together, purposefully thought about random things like the small crack in the windowpane I was leaning against or the faded parking lines in the lot below. It didn't work; my body still trembled with unspent energy.

I closed my eyes and saw Maddy's face smiling at me through the darkness. I thought back to the last time I'd seen her happy. It was the morning of the accident. I was talking to myself, muttering about how the admissions board at RISD would have to be out of their minds to accept me. I'd balled up my fifth attempt at the same sketch and tossed it at the door, not even knowing Maddy was standing there, watching me, listening to me. She caught it and opened it, studied the drawing before tucking it into her back pocket.

"Perfection isn't everything," she said as she turned and walked away. "I think the flaws are what make it perfect."

Without opening my eyes, I started drawing her. The deep set of her eyes, the dimple in our left cheeks, that crazy strand of hair she was always fighting into place. Her image flowed through me onto the paper as if drawing her kept me connected to her, bringing a small piece of Maddy back to me.

The doors above me opened and I heard footsteps.

"Hey," a familiar voice added.

I looked up and saw Josh standing there. He looked confused instead of angry at me. He was a little thinner and paler than usual, but it didn't matter because just seeing him brought the sense of calm I'd been sitting here struggling to regain.

God, I missed him.

I followed the line of his shoulder down his arm, then to his hand, intertwined with somebody else's. I didn't have to look up to know whose it was. Kim's.

Jealousy, as thick and tainting as bile, rose in me and I winced. I had to swallow it down and remind myself who I *really* was, how much more I meant to Josh than she did. I'd always liked Josh, figured eventually we'd become more than just friends. But I never had the courage to tell Josh how I really felt, and he never made a move, so I waited, comforted by the fact that even though Josh was technically dating Kim, he spent all of his time with me.

I'd watched Kim for the last few months, laughing as she tried to flirt her way into Josh's life. She had succeeded, or at least had gotten as close to Josh as she could. She came along when we went out for pizza and had been dragged to my house to watch movies or hang out. She even sat through our weekly anime meetings. The only difference I could see between her and me was that she had to share his popcorn and soda at the movies while I always had my own.

But I'd never felt threatened by her before. I'd watched her snuggle into him at the lunch table, thread her fingers through his hair on my couch, and giggle at his obviously lame jokes, and it had never bothered me. Until now. Now, when I had no claim to Josh in *any* capacity—not as a friend, not as a boyfriend—now I felt threatened.

"Hey," I said back, my eyes still locked on their hands. Anything more and I was afraid I'd slip, say something or do something to crack the fragile control I was desperately clinging to.

Josh tugged his hand free of Kim's and dug it into his front pocket, then rocked back on his heels so he was farther away from her. Kim eased herself in to his side and looked up at him, her gaze darting between Josh and me as if trying to figure us out.

"Hi, Maddy." There was a forced cheerfulness in Kim's voice. It was the same tone I'd heard her use on Josh when she was flirting, the same shy grin I'd seen her flash when she was trying to convince him to go to the movies alone, just the two of them.

"I'm sorry about your sister," she said. "I used to hang out with her. She was nice."

Kim reached her hand out to touch me, some fleeting gesture meant to show her condolences, but I flinched. She hadn't hung out with me; she hung out with Josh. She didn't know me, and I doubted she knew Josh. Not like I did anyway. And I sure didn't want her sympathy. I wanted her gone. Away from him. Away from us.

"You didn't hang out with Ella. You didn't know anything about her."

She paled at my words. "What?"

I shook my head, wondering why I was considering explaining myself. I was Maddy now, and I knew for a fact *she* didn't care about Kim or Josh, where they went on their date last Friday, or how far they'd gone last time they made out. To Maddy, they were insignificant people who weren't worthy of her time.

"You and Josh . . ." My voice slipped on his name, my own more casual tone seeping in. I slammed my mouth shut, shocked that I'd done it. I'd never let my voice slip when I was playing Maddy. Never. Not when we were kids pretending to be each other for fun, not during the countless times I took her tests, and not once since the accident. Why now, why here when I had so much to lose?

Kim looked at Josh, fluttered her hand between us in a futile attempt to get him to say something, to call me out for being rude to her. He didn't. He stood there, his fists bunching in his jeans pockets as he watched me, studied me. He'd heard the slip in my voice; I knew he had.

"Kim," he said, his eyes still totally focused on me, "can you give me and . . . uh—can you give us a minute alone?"

She hesitated, then opened her mouth to protest. Josh held up his hand, cutting her off. "Please, I'll meet you in the cafeteria in a few."

She whispered something into his ear before giving him a kiss. He turned his head, and she caught his cheek.

I laughed. I couldn't help it. For once today it was nice to see somebody else getting the short end of the stick.

Josh gave me that same irritated glare I'd seen a thousand times. One that told me to knock it off. I did, settled into the window seat, and watched as Kim walked away.

22

Josh waited until Kim was gone, then waited a bit longer before he spoke. "You okay?"

"Yeah . . . sorry about that," I said, waving in the direction of the door Kim had sulked through. "I shouldn't have been mean to her. It was wrong."

"That's not what I meant." He took a step closer and repeated his question slowly. "Are. You. Okay?"

"Yes . . . no . . . I mean . . ." I wavered, unsure of how to answer. My shoulder no longer ached, and most of my bruises had faded to a pale yellow. My left wrist was still in a cast, and I had a red line above my right eye where they'd stitched my skin together. But other than that, I was fine.

Physically anyway.

"I'm good."

Josh nodded but didn't move, rather, shifted the weight

of his backpack to his other shoulder and continued to watch me.

"What do you want?" I asked him.

"Your sister . . . Ella used to sit here," he said as he dropped his backpack to the floor and nudged my feet so he could climb up onto the sill next to me. He picked up the notebook I'd been drawing in, instinctively flipping to the back cover as he took in my drawing and compared it to the living, breathing version sitting next to him.

"Not bad," he said as he tucked it into his own bag. "The shading is a bit off, but my guess is, you're out of practice."

Jerk! The shading was nearly perfect. I went to call him out but stopped myself short and played along. "Yup, about four years. I haven't picked up a drawing pencil since junior high. That was Ella's thing, not mine."

He shook his head as if daring me to continue. "I know. Trust me, I know."

"You think you know everything about Ella?"

"I know I do. In fact, whenever she was upset about something or was trying to hide, this is where she'd go."

I cursed silently to myself. I'd known that. That was probably why I was sitting here. It was safe. Familiar.

"So what?" I said, aiming for indifference. "My sister and I had a lot in common. We were twins. Identical twins."

Josh chuckled at that, the who-are-you-trying-to-kid

sound that used to make me smile. Now it irritated the crap out of me. "Not since I've known you. Different friends. Different classes. Different everything. Same DNA, I guess, but that's about it."

He pulled me away from the wall I was leaning against, his eyes staring at the beige cinder block behind me. I followed his line of sight, knowing what I'd find.

"She drew that, you know," he said as he inched closer to me to get a better look at the drawing I'd sketched on the wall our freshman year. "The first day I met her, the day you introduced me to her, I found her sitting here drawing on the wall after school. I think she'd been crying, although she insisted she wasn't. Blamed her red eyes on allergies, I think."

I heard the humor in his voice as he recalled the excuse I'd fed him. I *had* been crying. I was hurt and confused and lonely.

"I asked her what was wrong, and she said nothing. Eventually I got her to tell me."

"What'd she say?" I asked, already knowing the answer.

"You. She didn't understand what she'd done, why you didn't want to hang out with her anymore," Josh said.

I shrugged. He was right; back then I didn't know. Still didn't, I guess. I simply learned not to care about it so much.

"I told her not to let it bother her, that Alex was exactly the same way, but she never stopped caring about you or worrying what you thought of her. She was always doing things to make your life easier. Even the night of the accident . . . Ella came for you, dropped everything and came to pick you up when you called."

"Whatever," I said, and jumped down off the sill. Sitting here watching him slowly poke at me, unknowingly reminding me of who I was, wasn't going to help.

I'd made it down a few steps when he stopped me, his hand reaching out for my shoulder. I let it linger there, let myself soak up his familiar warmth before shrugging him off. I could feel myself shaking, the fine tremor of fear working its way through my body. I didn't turn around to meet his eyes. Not because I was scared or guilty, but because I knew he'd see straight through me.

"I have class." It took an enormous amount of energy to get those three words out and even then my voice sounded weak . . . fragile.

"She was my best friend," he said softly. "I knew her better than she probably knew herself."

"What are you trying to say?"

He hesitated, and I could hear him sighing, as if he was carefully measuring his words. "Nothing. But if you ever want to talk about her . . . to remember *who* she was and what I loved about her, don't go to Alex. You come find me."

I'd known it'd be hard—pretending to be someone else. I'd have to keep my guard up, watch what I said and how I dressed, and make sure I answered questions incorrectly so that I could maintain Maddy's *average* performance in school. But in the end, or so I'd convinced myself, it'd be worth it. I could spare Mom and Dad, even Alex, from losing Maddy. What I hadn't figured into the equation was Josh.

I'd known Josh for three years and had spent nearly every spare minute of each day with him. He knew the way I walked, the way my right eye would twitch when I was angry, and he even knew about the string bracelet I refused to take off regardless of how nasty it got.

He reached for my hand, pushed up the sleeve of my shirt, and ran his fingers across my wrist. I let him, stood there silently knowing the proof he was looking for wasn't there. The ER staff had cut off that ratty old string bracelet along with everything else I was wearing that night.

I'd spent hours those first few days at home trying to re-create it. But no matter how many times I tried, I couldn't get the colors to match up the way I wanted, the way I remembered. Even using brand-new thread the colors seemed duller, less vibrant. I kept the poor replica anyway. It was tucked in the back pocket of my jeans, a small reminder of what I was purposefully giving up.

His hand clenched around my wrist, my fingers going cold beneath his grip. He could stare at the spot for hours, could will that tiny bit of evidence into place, but it was never going to happen. I was Maddy Lawton now. The popular, cherished, and adored Maddy Lawton.

I'd never lied to Josh, never had a reason to. And I wasn't planning on starting today. "I know everything I need to know about Ella," I said as I yanked my wrist free and walked away. "Everything."

23

The tight rein I had on my emotions fell away the instant the door closed behind me. I could feel myself trembling, and I was torn between wanting to scream with rage and cry with hopelessness. I didn't know what to do, who I was, or where I was going, and I had to figure it out in front of a school full of gossiping peers.

"Maddy?" Her name fluttered across my mind, the familiarity of it crushingly present and distant at the same time.

"Maddy?" Mom said again. Her hand grazed my chin as she lifted my face to look at her. I felt the sting of tears threatening to break free. I wanted nothing more than to run and hide. "What's wrong? Why are you home from school?"

What I came out with was a lie. "I got a headache and felt sick to my stomach."

I don't know whether it was relief or fear I saw in my

mother's eyes, but she kicked into action, cleared the table of the hospital bills she was studying, and motioned for me to sit down.

"Take one of these," she said as she shook a pain pill out of the bottle and into my hand. "I'm going to fix you something to eat."

I wasn't hungry, and no amount of painkillers was going to still the chaos that cluttered my mind. What I wanted was answers—clues—a road map for how to navigate my sister's life.

"I'm going to lie down," I said, heading for the stairs.

"After you eat," Mom insisted. She waved me back in and opened a can of soup. "Did you drive home? Does the school know you left early? Does Alex know you left early?"

I said yes, hoping my answer to the first question would carry over to the other two. I hadn't told anybody I was leaving. I climbed down off that windowsill and kept going until I found myself behind the wheel of my sister's new car, driving the same roads I had that night, my mind lost in an abyss of unanswered questions, until I found myself here, still pretending, but now at home.

Instinctively, I pulled out the chair I always used and sat down. If Mom noticed, she didn't say anything, but Bailey did. He came up to me and laid his head down on my lap, his tail wagging. He let out a low whine and started nosing my hand, practically climbing into my lap when I petted his head. I pushed him down, but he kept coming back, refusing to leave me alone.

Mom dumped the soup into a bowl, not bothering to measure the amount of water before she poured it in and placed the soup in the microwave. I counted the seconds, then heard her open and close the microwave door before she dropped an ice cube in and placed the bowl in front of me.

That was what I needed to do. In order to survive, I needed to focus on the ordinary stuff in Maddy's life. The color of her nail polish. The placement of pictures on her mirror. The way her shoes always matched her belt. If I concentrated on the little stuff, the pretty stuff, eventually things would get better, being Maddy would become easier.

I took two spoonfuls and then, ignoring my mother's pleas that I eat more, stood up and headed for the stairs. The headache I had lied about was quickly appearing, burrowing its way into my head, taking with it any sense of control I had left. I grabbed the tiny white pill Mom had given me and let it dissolve in my mouth, the bitter taste a stinging distraction before I swallowed. I'd give it ten minutes to work, then I'd add some NyQuil and sleep my way through this living nightmare.

The door to my room was open, the light on my nightstand casting an odd glow across the floor. My iPod was in the player, the random mix of songs each carrying with it a memory long buried. I pushed the door wider and walked in. I hadn't been in my old room this morning, yet my iPod . . . Ella's iPod was playing music.

My pillow was gone and the contents of the box of

personal effects the police had given my parents was strewn across the bed. Next to everything lay dozens of my sketchpads, some going as far back as elementary school, when my artwork consisted of nothing more than a stick figure with a balloon for a head. I gathered them up in my arms, a few stray drawings falling to the floor. Circling the room, I looked for a place to hide them, to store them out of sight. The last thing I wanted was to look at them, to find myself absorbed in the sketches I'd poured my heart into as I replayed a past that was no longer mine.

The door at the end of the hall clicked shut, and I dropped my stuff on the bed, worried that Mom had been watching me. I knocked on her door and waited a half second to see if she would answer before I quietly turned the knob.

Mom didn't hear me come in. She was busy picking up stuff from her floor. My pillow was there and my favorite pair of jeans—the ones I wore so often that they were frayed at the bottom and had a hole in one knee. My most recent sketchbook was there, the one that had the drawings I'd been working on for RISD. She had one torn out, half-taped to black cardboard matting, a glass frame sitting next to it.

I watched her for a minute, her hands shaking as she struggled to tear a strip of tape off. Tissues littered her floor and five half-drunk cups of coffee ringed the area she was sitting in. Mom was exhausted—I could tell by looking at her—but fighting sleep.

"What are you doing?" I asked.

Mom looked up at me, her gaze distant, as if she were seeing something that wasn't there. The smile that eventually came to her face was sad and full of haunted hope. I knew that look, understood it more than she knew. Every morning when I woke up, for those first few seconds when my mind was still hazy with sleep, I would forget that Maddy was gone. Within minutes my mind would clear, reality setting back in, leaving me with the dark truth. Yet I lived for those precious few seconds, longed for them every time I closed my eyes.

"I'm sorry," I choked out. I had no idea what to say, no idea how to wipe away the torture I could see flooding her eyes. "I'd do it differently if I could. You know that, right?"

That wasn't a lie. I didn't want to be Maddy. I wanted her back. I'd redo that entire night. I'd answer the phone the first time Maddy called. I'd refuse to go get her. I'd text Josh and make him bring her home. I'd do any of those "what ifs" were I given the chance.

"It's not your fault, Maddy." Mom quickly dried her eyes, the stoic mask she'd worn for weeks sliding back into place. I couldn't help but wonder how long she'd been doing that, how many nights these past weeks she'd handed me a bowl of soup and promised me it was going to be okay, then retreated to her room to silently lose it.

She reached out to touch me, to wipe the tears I didn't know were falling from my cheeks. I backed away, deserving no part of her comfort. "I miss her and I don't know how to bring her back. I'm trying, I am, but it's not working. I'm constantly screwing up."

"No, you're not." I turned around at my father's voice. I watched as his eyes drifted past me to my mom, then to the stack of baby pictures she had balanced on one of my journals. His next words drifted out on a sigh, and I didn't know if they were meant for me or Mom. "You're doing fine, better than anyone expected."

"Why are you here?" I asked.

His briefcase was still in his hand, his tie loosened but still on. He'd gone to work the Monday after the burial service and went in early and worked late each night.

"The school called and said you skipped most of your classes. I called Alex, he couldn't find you either. I tried your cell, but you didn't pick up."

I pulled my phone from my pocket and stared at it. Nine missed calls. Four from Dad. Four from Alex. And one from Josh. I hadn't heard it ring. Ignoring the rest, I clicked on Josh's number. No message. No nothing.

Dad's hand wrapped around mine, squeezing gently to get my attention. "We need to talk about this, Maddy. The three of us need to work our way through this."

I yanked my hand free and started to walk away. "Maddy, wait," Dad called after me. "You can't keep doing this. You can't pretend everything is fine."

"Do you ever wish Ella had lived?" It was an unfair question to ask, as there was no right answer. If they said yes, if they said they wished Ella was alive, it's not like I

166

was going to come clean and reveal who I was. And if they said no, if they said they were happy it was Maddy who had survived—either way their answer would crush me, leave me feeling more guilty, more trapped than before. But I asked it anyway. "Do you ever wonder what it would've been like if I had died and not her?"

Mom paled, and Dad took a step back. Neither of them spoke. They stared at me as if calculating what the proper response was supposed to be. That silence, that pause in time and the look of dread on their faces had me wondering if they'd thought about it, if I'd asked the one question that they secretly agonized over.

"Never," Dad replied. "I wouldn't trade you, *either* of you, for the other."

"Maddy, please." I heard the plea in Mom's voice, knew that if I looked up, I'd see tears to match. "I've lost your sister. I can't lose you, too."

I don't know what possessed me to say it. Perhaps I was looking for a way to tell them the truth without having to admit it, without the risk of them actually understanding what I was saying. Without giving a second thought to my words, I raised my eyes to meet my mother's and said, "I'm already gone. I died that night on the side of that road with my sister."

24

I walked the two miles to the cemetery. To my sister's grave. To my grave. It was cold and starting to rain. I'd left my coat at home on the kitchen chair, but none of that mattered. I didn't feel it—not the sting of the rain as it turned to ice or my hands shaking as they hung limply by my side. I kept walking, oblivious to everything.

I knew where the marker was. It was buried five rows deep amid a couple hundred other stones. They laid it yesterday. My parents asked if I wanted to go with them to see it last night, but I didn't. There was something about seeing my name carved into granite that I didn't think I was quite ready to handle.

But I hadn't come here today for visual proof of what I had done, of the finality of the lie I had spun. I'd come to talk to the sister whose life I was trying desperately to figure out.

"Hey." I ran my hand across the smooth stone, taking with it a puddle of water. I studied it for a second, watched the drops roll off my fingers and onto the ground. I couldn't help but wonder if she was cold and wet, if she had been cold and wet the night the paramedics pulled her from the heated car and into the dark night.

I looked at the ground, my eyes following the line of the grass. They'd put it back in place, like a carpet they'd unrolled, but it was dying, brown and brittle. The lines where they'd peeled back the original sod gaped, as if it was retreating into itself, as if the grass had tried and failed miserably at reseeding itself.

Kind of like me.

"It's raining again," I said as I sank to the ground. The wet grass soaked the legs of my jeans. I watched, mesmerized as the light blue faded to dark, the edges inching out until I could feel the cold settling into my bones. Only then, when a violent chill had me moving to my heels, did I speak again. "It seems like it's always raining when I see you. Always cold."

I hadn't been here since the day of her burial. I had refused each morning when Mom asked me if I wanted to go. She thought it might make things easier, that perhaps it would bring me some closure. Closure wasn't what I needed. Advice was.

"I went to school today. Alex is great. He's helping me figure my way around the stares," I said, leaving out the part about him trying to kiss me the night before. Dead or not, I wasn't quite sure how to bring up that topic with my sister.

"I still don't get why you hang out with Jenna, though. She's selfish and mean, and I don't think she even likes you. I'm quite sure she's actually working behind your back to screw you over," I said as if Maddy was sitting right there next to me, as if we were having a conversation about something as mundane as what flavor cake we were going to have on our eighteenth birthday. "Alex told me that her parents are going to lose the house and her brother had to drop out of school to get a job. That kind of sucks for him."

I swallowed the tinge of pity I felt for Jenna. I didn't want to understand her behavior. I had no intention of forgiving her for years' worth of snide remarks and intentional cruelty. Family problems aside, she was still mean and selfish.

"I think you got an A on your Lit test," I said, laughing. "No worries, that won't happen again. I'll be sure to make enough mistakes to get you a solid C next time around."

"Next time," I muttered to myself. Those two words sounded foreign and remote. I'd been so focused on getting through one day, one hour, one minute as Maddy that I hadn't thought about the simple fact that I'd have to get up and do it over again at school, in public, tomorrow.

I paused, shaking my head in disgust as I realized what I was doing. I could almost hear her scolding me, going on about how if I wanted to, I could be as pretty and popular as her. I'd disagree with her, remind her that she was the beautiful one, always had been.

I thought about the first time we had that recurring argument. It was in freshman year and it lasted three days—until Mom finally stepped in and told us either to knock it off or risk losing our phones for a week. Dad pulled me aside that Saturday after dinner. He sat me down in his study and took out his wallet; he showed me the pictures he'd accumulated of us over the years. They were cheesy-looking school pictures with fake fall foliage or blue backgrounds. He had one for each year we'd been in school.

I'd flipped through those pictures, groaning at the one where a gaping hole replaced my two front teeth, then tossed them back at him, completely confused as to what ten years of school photos had to do with anything.

He put his wallet on the desk next to his keys and told me to think about what Maddy had said and the words she had used. I thought about it for a half second, then left the room vowing to hate her forever.

"I'm an idiot. We're identical twins." I whispered those words to her now, finally getting what both Maddy and Dad had been trying to say.

"I miss you. I know we weren't getting along lately, but I figured eventually we'd work it out. I never imagined we wouldn't get the chance."

I picked up a strand of dead grass and started peeling the fine threads apart. When one was shredded, I tossed it to the ground and started on another. "Mom's losing it, and Dad thinks I need to talk to a shrink. Alex agrees."

There was her sweet voice again, as clear as day, asking me what I'd *expected* to happen. The few times I'd come to her with a problem, she'd done that—rolled her eyes and told me to open my eyes and watch, stop thinking so much and watch how other people did it, then figure it out.

"Mom had my drawings. She was trying to frame one. It was a crappy one I had left over from my application to art school."

I thought about my mother's tears, the look of pure anguish that had clouded her eyes. I'd done that. In every way possible, I'd done that to her.

"Dad's working a lot," I continued. "Both he and Mom think the three of us need to talk"—I paused and waved my hand around the damp ground I was sitting on, my eyes landing on my own name etched in granite—"about this."

Her words echoed through my mind with bittersweet clarity. *And let me guess, Ella. You don't want to talk about it. You want to curl up with your sketch pad and forget it happened.*

"You're right." Talking about it wouldn't make it go away, wouldn't bring Maddy back. It would only make the pain clearer.

I reached out, my hand meeting the cold, hard side of the gravestone. "I don't want to remember any of it," I said, as tears pooled in my eyes. "I want to change it. I want you back."

"Have you talked to anybody about it? Since the day you woke up in that hospital bed, have you spoken of it?"

My whole world stopped at the sound of his voice. Everything froze as I fought to speak the lie I'd entrenched myself in. "Josh, it's not—"

"Don't," he said as he held his hand up for me to stop. "Don't say that I'm wrong or that I don't know who I'm looking at."

I shook my head, not knowing what to say. "I can't do this now. Not with you."

"Not with anybody if you have your way." Josh backed up and pulled a wrinkled piece of paper from his pocket. His gaze was fixed on mine, like he was giving me one last chance to say he was wrong. He mumbled something under his breath when I stayed quiet, then dropped the piece of paper and walked away.

25

It was wrinkled, like it had been crumpled into a ball, then smoothed out and neatly folded. The paper was thin, blue-lined, the jagged pieces from where it had been torn from a notebook still hanging on.

I carefully unfolded it and smoothed it across the granite marker. The dampness started to seep through the paper, curling the edges and blotching the middle. But I didn't need it to be perfect to recognize it. I knew what it was—a crude drawing I'd made thousands of times before. I didn't remember sketching this particular version, but I recognized the length of the lines, the gentle curve of the strokes, the darkened pressure marks where each line started. It was one of my drawings, no question about that.

I wondered where Josh had gotten it and why he was carrying it around. I had fifty of these at home, each one better than this. Why would he bother to keep this one?

"Maddy?" I swung around at the sound of my father's voice. "You okay?"

No was the truthful answer, but I shrugged. "I'm fine. What are you doing here?"

"Looking for you. I tried Alex's first, thinking maybe you would've gone there when you left the house."

"I didn't," I said. Alex's was the last place I would go. He was half the reason I had left school early—I couldn't figure him out and was terrified I'd screw up.

"I passed Josh on the way in," Dad continued. "You know he comes here every day like me."

I nodded, not sure what to say. I knew Dad stopped here on his way home from work. As for Josh . . . well, I wasn't exactly surprised.

Before the accident, I'd hardly ever lied to my dad. Now it seemed all I did was lie to him. To everybody. "Josh wanted to talk to Ella," I said, vaguely sticking to the truth.

"Is that why you're here? To talk to your sister?"

"Yes."

"I was hoping maybe you could talk to me," he said, "but you left before we had a chance."

"Because there is nothing to talk about."

Typical of Dad, he nodded and changed his line of questioning, coming at me from a different angle. "Everything okay at school?"

"Yup. I didn't feel well, so I went home." He knew that was a lie. I'd insisted I felt good enough to return to school last night when we argued about it. They wanted me to take a few more days, meet with the counselor before I went back.

"Your mother is worried about you. I'm worried about you."

"I'm fine, Dad. Honestly. But I don't want to talk about it. Not yet."

"Are you talking to Alex at least?"

Alex had stopped asking me about the accident after my first day home. I'd clam up or sometimes cry whenever he mentioned it at the hospital. By the time I'd gotten home, he probably figured it was safer not to ask. "Yeah. I guess."

We stood there, neither one of us knowing what to say to break the heavy silence that surrounded us. The rain had nearly stopped, a few scattered drops staining the paper. My eyes drifted to the drawing I clutched in my hand.

"What do you have there?" Dad asked as he reached for the drawing.

I gave it to him and watched as he studied it. He folded it neatly and gave it back to me, his gaze turning to the gravestone behind us.

"She loved to draw. I swear she learned how to use a crayon before mastering a fork," Dad said, chuckling. I hadn't heard that sound in weeks. It made me smile and remember how when I was a kid, I'd made him enough drawings to completely cover his office walls. Every single one of them courtesy of Crayola.

"I miss her." It was the first honest thing I'd said to him since I woke up in the hospital. I missed her hogging the shower in the morning and the smell of nail polish remover overtaking the bathroom. I wanted to hear her yelling for me to come down for dinner and teasing me when I tried to explain to Mom why I had no desire to go to prom.

And I missed me—Ella. I missed sitting at the lunch table with Josh, laughing to myself as Kim vied for his attention. I missed our Saturday-afternoon movie marathons and his moronic texts asking me how to handle Kim.

"I miss her too. More than you can ever know."

Those last words were whispered. I don't think he intended to speak them aloud, but they stunned me all the same. I couldn't help myself—I asked, "What do you miss most about her?"

He stepped back, his face going pale. "I don't blame you, Maddy. Nobody blames you. Please don't think—"

"I don't," I interrupted. "I'm trying to figure her out. Ella, you know. What people thought of her. Who she really was."

"Quiet," was Dad's first response. "Beautiful, and quiet, and so incredibly talented, but you already know that, don't you?"

I thought about asking him what, exactly, he meant. Luckily, I didn't have to. He answered before I could speak. "She was your twin sister, Maddy. I remember when you two were little. You were inseparable, even insisting on sleeping in the same room, in the same bed. You probably knew her better than anybody."

"Umm, yeah, not so much anymore."

Dad shook his head. He knew we'd grown apart these last few years. Everybody who spent any time with us knew that. "She's the same Ella she was back then."

"Maybe," I said, hoping that was true, that somewhere beneath this lie was the real me. I picked at the tattered edges of the picture I was holding, mindlessly dropping the shreds of paper to the ground. "Dad, have you ever made a mistake, done something that you didn't intend to but couldn't take back?"

"Of course. Everybody has, but you can't change the past, Maddy. You can't change what happened." He pulled me into his arms, and I knew he thought I was referring to the accident, that I was finally starting to talk. "You can't go back. You have to try to make peace with what happened and move forward. We all do."

His arms tightened around me as if he was willing me to believe him, to forgive myself and move on. I pulled away. It felt wrong to be forgiven.

"If you are looking to learn more about your sister, perhaps you should start with Josh. He was her best friend. He spent more time with her than any of us."

"Yeah, maybe."

"Go," Dad said, nudging me toward the road. "Go talk to him. He's hurting as much as you."

26

I traced a circular pattern on the driveway with my foot. I could see the pavement through the spot I'd cleared, the puddle of rain trying to ease its way back as I continued to swipe it away. I'd been standing in Josh's driveway for over twenty minutes trying to talk myself into knocking on his door, and I still couldn't find the courage to move.

"Stop being a chicken, Ella. It's just Josh." I took one long, fog-filled breath and made my feet move, willed them to walk those last few steps up the slate walkway to his front door.

The bright motion-sensor porch lights came on as soon as I hit the bottom step, announcing my arrival to anyone sitting in the living room. I couldn't even apologize to Josh in privacy.

Mrs. Williams opened the door as my hand was about to

ring the doorbell. "El—" She stopped mid-name and took a step back, the color draining from her face as she grabbed the doorknob for support. I couldn't blame her. The rain had washed any trace of makeup, and my hair hung in matted locks around my face. Like this, I guess I did look like me.

I should've said something, corrected her initial reaction or walked past her, but I couldn't. I just stood there, my feet glued to the porch, my mouth forgetting how to form words.

"Maddy?"

I didn't know whether she was asking me what I wanted or questioning who I was, so I opted for number one. "Hi, Mrs. Williams. Is Josh here?"

She stepped aside and motioned me in. "He's upstairs. I'll go get him."

"No." The last thing I needed was an audience. "I'll find him."

I made for the stairs, forgetting that Maddy had never been in this house. She'd picked me up here a few times. She would sit at the curb and honk her horn until I came out, but she'd never been closer than that. She wouldn't know which room was Josh's, never mind jog up the stairs like she owned the place. "Uh . . . which room is his?"

"Last one on the right. You sure you don't want me to go get him?"

I shook my head and took the first few steps two at a time. "Maddy?" Mrs. Williams's voice halted me, and I

turned, my eyes dancing across the front door before settling on her. There was still time to leave, still time to
walk out that door and keep pretending.

"I'm sorry about your sister," she finally said.

"Me too," was what I came out with—a weak, pathetic
me too.

The upstairs hall was empty, the lights off except the
one flowing out from underneath Josh's door. I knew
where the light switches were, knew that if I turned to my
left there would be three switches, the middle one a dim-
mer. I didn't bother to flick one on; I didn't need it. This
was my second home. I could navigate my way up the stairs
to his room with my eyes closed.

I walked the hall on instinct alone, my feet knowing
exactly how many steps to take, my hand automatically
knowing which door to tap on.

"It's open," he called.

I slowly turned the brass knob. Part of me knew I
would regret this—admitting to a lie I had every intention
of continuing to live. The other part of me, the part guid-
ing my hand, knew I owed Josh an explanation.

I opened the door enough to peek in, still wavering
between staying and leaving. He was sitting cross-legged
on the floor, his History notes sprawled out in front of
him.

I shook my head in self-disgust. I'd spent countless
nights here on that floor, in that exact same position, por-
ing over Physics notes or copying Latin translations. This

was the same Josh I had always known, the same one I went to in the past with stupid problems. Why did I want to hide from him now?

He looked up from his homework, his expression guarded. "Hey, Ella."

I'd heard him utter my name a thousand times before. Heard him yell it at me last month when we were fighting over which indie film to feature in the anime club's October newsletter, and whisper it to me the next day in school when he was trying to get my attention during class so he could apologize. But never before had it sounded so flat . . . so matter-of-fact.

"What have I done?" With those whispered words I lost it, the tears I'd been fighting finally fell, poured from my eyes as my entire body shook violently with sobs. Josh's reaction was instantaneous. He got up and closed the door before dragging me close and pulling me into his arms. I didn't fight him as he guided my head to his chest. I no longer had the strength or the desire to lie to the one person who'd ever truly known me.

The steady, rhythmic beat of his heart thrummed beneath my cheek as his palm moved soothingly up and down my back. His cheek warmed the top of my head and the constant lull of his voice was peaceful, perfect. For the first time since the accident, I felt safe and warm, and I wanted to stay here, locked in his arms, forever.

It seemed like hours before my sobs quieted to a whimper. His shirt was soaked from my tears, his hands shaking on my back. I didn't pull away to see if he was crying. I didn't want to know.

"You're soaking wet," he said as he brushed at his now-damp shirt.

"What?" Surprise and confusion swirled inside me. I had just admitted to pretending to be dead and taking over my sister's life, and the only thing he thought to comment on was my wet clothes?

I stared down at my shoes. They were squishy, the leather strap leaving a smudge across the top of my feet. "I walked here. It was still drizzling when I left the cemetery, but it has stopped now."

"Here," Josh said. He stripped off his sweatshirt and gave it to me. "None of my jeans will fit you, but I've got a pair of sweatpants you can borrow."

I took the sweatshirt, and he dug through his dresser for a clean pair of pants. He handed them to me and looked at the floor until I was completely changed.

On top of my pile of wet clothes, I laid the earrings and the locket I'd found in Maddy's jewelry box, plus the five thousand silver bangles I'd put on this morning.

"You look like you now," he said, and I smiled. For the first time in weeks, I actually felt like me.

"How'd you figure it out?" I asked.

"Figure what out?"

"How did you figure out it was me . . . that I was Ella and not Maddy? I mean, Alex hasn't figured it out. Not even my parents have questioned it."

"Yeah, well, that's Alex. Your parents . . ." Josh paused and shrugged as if he couldn't explain that one. "They're upset, probably grieving too much to look that closely."

"Yeah, maybe," I said, quite sure that wasn't the case. They had the daughter they wanted, or at least that's what I was telling myself. "But how did *you* figure it out?"

"You told me."

"What? No I didn't." In fact, I had gone out of my way to make sure I hadn't let anything slip in front of him. With the exception of that small slip of my voice in the stairwell today, I'd stayed completely in part.

"You have that drawing I left in the cemetery?"

"Yeah." I pulled it out of my pocket and handed it to him.

He unfolded it much the way I had, but using his leg to smooth it out. "This told me," he said, waving it in my direction.

"I don't get it. I've drawn hundreds of those. What's so special about this one?"

"Exactly," he said. "I . . . we have AP English in the same room as Maddy. One period later, after she has American Lit. I found it crumpled up by the desk you were sitting in. I wouldn't have thought anything of it, but you've been drawing that same tree since the day I met you. You do it whenever you zone out."

He was right. That gnarly old willow tree sat in my front yard. It had been beaten down a few times by winter storms and the occasional hurricane. That's why I always

184

drew it—it either cracked a limb or lost a branch every week. It was always changing, a constant, inanimate object that gave me something new to capture each day.

"You found this on the floor?" I remembered finishing my test early, rereading my answers, and still having a good ten minutes left to kill. I must have drawn it while I was waiting for the bell to ring, mindlessly putting pencil to paper.

"Umm hmm, and I'd like it back if you don't mind."

"Why?" I asked, handing it to him.

"Because right now, or at least until you change your mind about this game you're playing, it's the only thing I have left of you."

27

I sat on his bed watching, waiting for him to say something. I thought about leaving. The anger I had seen less than thirty minutes ago was not something I wanted to deal with. But I'd wait him out, like he'd done for me.

"What do you remember about that night?" he finally asked.

"You don't understand, Josh."

"You're right, I don't."

"It didn't make any sense," I said, struggling to explain. "When I first woke up, I had no clue who I was . . . where I was. I didn't even know I had a sister. It was Alex who told me my name and what had happened."

Josh got up from his desk chair, hesitating for a minute before he sat down next to me on the bed. I could feel his breath on my cheek, the warmth of his hand as he nudged me to look at him. "And when you figured it out, when you finally got your memory back, why didn't you ask to see me? If you'd asked for me, had so much as said my name, they would've called me. Alex would've gotten me that first day, and *I* would've come, talked you out of this. Why didn't you ask for me?"

I stayed silent, my attention focused on a small rip in his comforter. I counted the threads, tried to gauge how many stitches it would take to repair it. Fifteen, I figured. Twenty, tops.

"Ella?" Josh said when I didn't respond. "Look at me. Look at me and tell me what you were thinking."

I blinked long and hard, then did as he asked, steeling myself for his anger before opening my eyes. It wasn't there. No anger, no hatred staring back at me, not even a bit of annoyance. What I saw was forgiveness and unwavering faith.

"I did ask for you."

"What? Wait, what are you saying?"

"I wasn't thinking. I woke up and everything hurt. Everything. He was there, holding my hand, whispering for me to wake up. And when I did, he was so happy to see her, like his whole—"

"And you didn't think I would be?" Josh interrupted. "You think that if I had any idea that it was *you* lying in that hospital bed I wouldn't have been there? That it wouldn't have been my hand you were holding, my eyes you saw first?"

"I didn't know who he was, who *I* was. And when he

187

told me, when Mom and Dad told me I was Maddy, I believed them."

"They told me you were dead, did you know that? When the police showed up at his house, Alex and I went to the ER. We had to pass Maddy's car on the way. It was still there, wrapped around the tree. The nurse at the front desk wouldn't let me see you. She told me nobody but your parents were allowed in the trauma room, and they weren't there yet. I kept thinking of you, hurt and alone."

"Don't," I begged. "Please don't." No amount of explanation was going to change this, no amount of anger or guilt could undo what I'd done.

"You know what Alex did?" Josh's gaze locked on mine, forcing me to see, to understand every single word he said. "He sat down. Right there in the hospital waiting room, he sat down and waited. He didn't argue with the nurse, or fight his way past the security guard to get to Maddy. He stayed there and didn't move, like he was frozen in place. You know what I did?"

I shook my head. I couldn't have spoken then even if I'd wanted to.

"I ignored them—the security guard, the nurse, everyone, and pushed my way through until some big orderly stopped me. But I got to see you, both of you, lying there hooked up to everything. The alarms on your sensors were going off. Hers . . . hers were silent."

I didn't remember any of that—not the emergency room, not the doctors, not Josh being there.

"You were both in the same room, your clothes piled up on the floor. I remembered the coat you had had on and the sweatshirt from RISD you never took off. I saw them in the pile of clothes. I knew you had them on when you came to pick up Maddy. I asked the nurse which one of you had been wearing *that*, and she pointed to Maddy. So that is where I went. Toward her. Toward the person I *thought* was you."

I nodded. I'd given her both in the car. She was cold and wet and shivering and I didn't know what else to do.

"One of the doctors asked if I knew you, and I gave him your names. He told me you were gone, that you had died instantly when you hit the tree. That you probably hadn't suffered. Like somehow that was supposed to make me feel better."

I knew what he meant. They'd told me the exact same thing, over and over. It didn't help. Not one single bit.

"At first I didn't believe them. I begged them to try again, to do something. But then the paramedic who pulled you—I mean Maddy—from the car came over and told me he'd done everything he could but she was already gone when they got there."

He paused and swiped his arm across his eyes. He wasn't crying but his eyes were heavy, and the hitch in his voice said he didn't want to relive this memory any more than I did.

"You know what I did, Ella?" I shook my head, and he continued. "I stayed there. I refused to leave. I sat there on the floor next to you—next to Maddy's body—until your parents arrived so you wouldn't be alone. Even then, I wouldn't go."

"Mom and Dad were so happy to see me when I woke up," I blurted out. "Everybody was. Alex was. I have never seen them like that, Josh, never seen any of them so scared and excited and relieved to see Maddy."

"You're kidding me, right? You based your decision to become your sister on your parents' reaction to seeing you? On Alex's relief that you were alive? I sat there for four hours holding Maddy's cold hand while Alex sat in the waiting room. In the waiting room, Ella! Being coddled by Maddy's friends. I was the one who was there with you . . . with her!" He waved his hand in the air, pissed. "It was me, not him, with you the whole time."

"But you didn't see my parents," I said, remembering Mom's tears, her whispered words about how she couldn't lose Maddy, too. "You didn't see Jenna or those people in the hall. Her friends. They were so happy that it was *her* who survived. I couldn't tell them it was a mistake, take back the one person they had begged fate to let live. Plus, I owed her. I'd killed her, Josh. My own sister. I killed her, and I owe her my life in return. I owe her that much."

Cursing my tears, I brushed them away. "She's the one they love. She's the one they were praying would survive."

"Is that what you think?" Josh asked, and I flinched at the fury I could hear in his voice. His entire body was vibrating, the tears I had seen earlier gone, replaced with pure, unadulterated anger.

"Answer me, Ella! Do you honestly think that your parents didn't . . . don't love you? That *our* group of friends wouldn't have spent two days in the hall waiting for you? That if everybody had a vote on who died that night, they would have chosen you over Maddy?"

I nodded. What else was I supposed to think?

Josh stood up and slammed his fist into the wall. Then he laughed, this broken cackle that had my emotions doing a complete one-eighty . . . going from guilt-ridden and confused to as irate as him.

"What's so funny?"

"You are." His amusement faded, the resentment I'd seen seconds ago slipping back into place. "They had to sedate your mom when she found out you were gone. That's why Alex was sitting with you. Not because he loved Maddy or wanted to be there, but because your dad made him, told him not to leave your side until he could get your mother under control and could come back and sit with you himself."

"That's not true," I said. There was no way that could be true. Mom adored Maddy. She went to her field hockey games, every one of them. She had pictures of Maddy lining her bureau and went out of her way to buy the healthy crap Maddy insisted on eating.

"And you know that how? You were out of it, Ella. For two days. You have no idea what went on. Take a good look at your mother now. You think she's happier believing Maddy is the one who survived? Are you saying that if she had a choice, your mom would've chosen your sister over you? If you honestly believe that, then you're an idiot."

"She did everything, *everything* for Maddy!" I yelled.

"Because you wouldn't let her do anything for you."

I flinched at his words. I didn't believe him. My parents, the kids at school, Alex, everybody loved Maddy more than me.

"This summer, when your mom wanted to get a family picture at the beach, what did you say?"

I remembered that. Mom had brought Josh along so that he could take the picture. I was angry about Dad refusing to let me drive to Savannah with Josh to see some art schools. I told them I didn't want to be in their family picture. Eventually Mom stopped arguing with me and handed me the camera, telling me to take the picture. I did, and now there was a picture of my parents and Maddy, without me, sitting on the mantel.

"How about the art exhibit at school last spring, the one where they displayed the sketch you were submitting to the national First Art Program. Why wasn't your mom there? Why weren't either of your parents there?"

I shook my head instead of answering. They weren't there because I never told them about it.

"Did you ever tell them you won?" he asked.

"Yes." They'd found out two weeks later when the award

192

and scholarship money came in the mail. Mom cried, and said she didn't understand why I would hide this from them, that I should be proud of what I'd accomplished and not hide it. Dad stomped around in silence.

"How about RISD? Do they know you applied early decision there?"

"No," I whispered. They didn't know about my application to art school. I'd just plugged Mom's e-mail address into the designated spot and sent it off, figuring I'd tell her and Dad if and when I got accepted.

"They didn't do anything for you because you made it pretty clear you didn't want their help," Josh said as he walked toward his door. He stopped with his hand on the knob, didn't look back as he spoke. "And as for nobody loving you, you are wrong there, too. I loved you. *I* would have chosen you."

He didn't give me a chance to respond. He just walked out. Left me sitting there staring after him, stunned and completely unable to move.

28

I hadn't considered Josh's feelings when I made my decision to become Maddy. I didn't consider a whole lot of things. It's not like I planned on becoming my sister. I just never corrected anybody when they assumed that's who I was.

With everybody beyond thrilled that she was alive, it had seemed easier to play along.

Distantly, I heard the front door slam shut, Josh's mother calling out after him. Knowing Josh, he was probably heading to the movie theater. He'd sneak in the exit door to watch whatever was playing, hiding out in the back row until he calmed down.

I stood up, wanting nothing more than to go with him. It didn't matter what was playing. It wasn't about actually watching the movie, but becoming invisible for a while. With him. But that was no longer an option for me. I had to go home, do a crappy job on my homework, then spend hours searching through fashion magazines so I could put together a Maddyesque-type outfit for school tomorrow.

I grabbed the pile of my wet clothes and toyed for half a second with the idea of putting them back on. But Josh's clothes were soft and warm, and for once, I wanted to be comfortable.

The house was quiet, the only noise coming from the kitchen. His mother's voice drifted over the sound of the oven timer and cupboards being opened and closed. She was talking to Josh's dad, or trying to at least. She'd gotten his voice mail, was asking him to call Josh when he landed and to figure out what was going on.

Quietly, I made my way through the living room, hoping to avoid any contact with Mrs. Williams. I'd nearly made it out of the house unnoticed, was less than half a step from the door, when I heard her call my name.

"Maddy." I faced her. She had the phone in one hand, a pot holder in the other. "Everything okay?"

"No," I said. Everything was so far from okay that even I couldn't make it work anymore.

She moved closer, nearly blocking my path.

"Sorry," was all I could think to say.

"For what?"

I shrugged. "I didn't know he felt that way about . . . about her."

She backed away from the door and motioned for me to pass. "He's lost so much already, Maddy. I think seeing you"—she paused, her eyes scanning me dressed in her son's clothes—"dressed like this doesn't help."

I didn't ask her to explain before I opened the door and left. I knew what she meant, knew what she was tactfully trying to tell me. *Leave her son alone.*

I pulled the hood of Josh's sweatshirt tighter around my head and clutched my still-wet clothes closer to my chest. It was getting dark, and it was colder than when I first arrived. And now I had to walk home.

"What are you doing here?" Kim sounded surprised, as if I was the last person she expected to see at Josh's house. Made sense, I guess. Ella was the one who practically lived here, not Maddy, and, well, Ella was dead.

"Nothing, just leaving," I said.

Kim walked around the small fence that separated her yard from Josh's. "You don't have to. I was just coming over to see if Josh wanted to hang out. You are welcome to stay. I mean, I know you probably have other things to do and Josh was Ella's friend not yours, but . . ."

I looked up and saw Josh standing there. Apparently I'd been wrong. He hadn't headed for the movies like I'd assumed. He was planning on spending time with Kim. I couldn't help but laugh. Back when I was Ella, I wouldn't have given Kim the time of day. She was jealous, and immature, and hung on Josh like a puppy to a mangled chew toy. I didn't get Josh's attraction to her. She was a sophomore without an ounce of artistic talent. Seriously, her idea of anime was *The Lion King.*

Plus, he loved me, not her. He'd just said so in his room.

Yeah, Ella would've ignored her, but I wasn't Ella anymore. I was Maddy.

Josh saw the resolve in my eyes and instantly knew what I was thinking. "Don't," he warned.

My eyes met his and a thousand unspoken words passed between us. There was an *I meant what I said upstairs*, and an *I'll help you figure this out*, and a final *Please, not in front of her*.

Kim watched, her face falling as she witnessed a connection she would never have with Josh. For a second, I felt bad for her. She saw it, saw that no matter what she did or how hard she tried, she could never hold him like I did. Even if I was dead, Josh belonged to me.

I nodded in Josh's direction and kept my mouth shut as I turned to walk away. It was the safest thing to do . . . the only thing to do.

"Wait," Josh said. "Let me get my keys, and I'll drive you home."

"No." I wanted to walk, needed to be alone to think things through before I had to answer any more of his questions.

I kept my eyes focused on the ground, ignoring Kim and Josh's arguing. He wanted to give me a ride, or at the very least walk me home. She thought Josh should call Alex so that he could pick me up. I didn't bother to tell her that Alex was the last person Josh wanted to see right now. Kim even offered to go get her own mother and make her drive me home.

"I'm fine," I said, putting up a hand to stop them. "I'll see you both tomorrow at school."

I knew Josh was following me. I'd heard the rumble of his car behind me minutes after I left his front yard. I smiled as he sped up and passed my house the second he knew I was safely inside. I liked knowing that after everything, he was still there watching out for me.

The house was quiet when I got home. The light was on above the stove and there was a half-eaten frozen pizza on the counter next to my now-cold bowl of soup. The coffeepot was full, the sink filled with mugs. I prayed Mom was asleep. I didn't want to answer her questions or apologize again for something I couldn't change. And I sure didn't want to talk about what had happened at Josh's.

I cut through the den on my way upstairs and saw Dad sitting in the living room. In the dim light, I could see the discarded newspaper by his feet and the glass of amber liquid in his hand.

"Where's Mom?" I asked.

"Upstairs. Asleep."

"She okay?" I don't know why I asked. I pretty much already knew the answer. Guess I wanted confirmation of how much she missed me—Ella—of how much they actually did care.

He shook his head and stood up, drained what was left of his drink before setting the glass down on the coffee table. "Maddy, we need to talk. You are closing yourself off. Your mom sees it. Alex sees it. I see it, and it scares us, Maddy. We can help you, but you need to let us in."

There were so many things I wanted to say, starting with *I'm sorry* and *I'm not Maddy*. But not yet. Not now. "I know, Dad, but not tonight," was what I actually said.

29

As selfish as it was, I felt better the next day because I wasn't the only one carrying around my complicated secret. Dad was gone by the time I got up, and Mom was still in bed. Probably for the best. I wasn't sure what, if anything, I wanted to say to her yet.

The kitchen was a mess, dishes were still in the sink and the coffeepot was still sitting on the counter, the bottom ringed with black sludge. At least Bailey had taken care of what was left of the pizza. The chicken soup though . . . somehow he'd managed to topple the bowl onto his head. He'd licked himself clean as best he could, but he was sticky, the fur on his head matted down and littered with tiny chunks of carrots. It was unusual for Mom to leave the kitchen like this. It was unusual for her to leave *anything* out of place.

I picked up the empty carton of creamer and tossed it

in the trash and was reaching for the dishwasher when I saw the e-mail printout. Moving an overturned mug aside, I picked up the page and swiped at the coffee stain on it. It was useless; the light brown stain was dried.

I recognized the e-mail address. It was from the department at RISD and addressed to both Mom and me.

I'd submitted the application the night Maddy died, the night I became her. I'd tried not to think about it since then. In fact, I'd nearly forgotten I'd even applied. Until now. Until the proof lay coffee-stained in my hand.

I didn't bother to read it, forced myself not to scan the first few lines to see what it said. I just shoved the e-mail into my bag and headed out the door, not wanting to be reminded of yet another thing I had failed to do right.

School was quiet, but I'd expected that. I'd come in early to avoid Alex. He'd have questions about why I left and why I wasn't returning his calls, and I didn't have any answers. Or not any that didn't involve a complicated set of lies.

I rounded the corner of the hallway and saw Josh standing there staring into his open locker. "Hey," I said.

His eyes flicked in my direction and I walked toward him. He was the only familiar thing in my life anymore, and I wanted to be close to him.

Josh waited until I stopped next to him before he looked at me, really looked at me, then shook his head.

"Back in the role, I see," he said, and returned his attention to his locker.

I knew what he meant. I had on leather boots and skinny jeans and three layers of shirts and sweaters that were strategically placed and itched like crazy. Crap, I was even getting better at doing my makeup. Thanks to two hours of practice last night, I'd only had one mishap with the mascara this morning, but luckily it wasn't waterproof.

"Yeah, for now," I said.

"Forever?"

I shrugged. That was the plan.

He slammed his locker shut, not a single book in his hands. "Yeah, well, I have class, and I have to go find Kim, so whatever."

"Wait." I reached out and grabbed his arm. I wasn't done talking to him. I hadn't *started* talking to him. His eyes zeroed in on the hand I had locked around his arm. He didn't flinch or try to shake me off. He stood there, hyperfocused on it.

Unsure of what to say, I let go and dropped my backpack to the floor. I unzipped it and pulled out the e-mail I'd stashed inside. "Here," I said, and handed it to him. "I don't know what it says. I was too scared to look."

Josh took the paper from my hands and stared at it much the same way I had in the kitchen. I saw the slight tremor in his hands, knew that he was as anxious as I was to see what it said.

"This isn't your e-mail address," he said.

I pushed it back in his direction when he tried to hand it to me. "I know. It's my mom's. She got it yesterday and printed it off." I left out the part about my mom not sleeping, about the circles under her eyes, the messy house, and the fact that I was quite sure she hadn't showered or changed since yesterday. Josh liked my mom. He thought she was sweet, always cooking him food or asking to see his latest drawing. I didn't want that to change. For either of them.

"So ask her what it says if you're so curious."

I took a step back at the harshness of his words. This was the plan. This was *always* the plan. We'd both dreamed about this since freshman year. We'd both applied early decision to the same school. We were going to open the replies together, each one reading the other's letter. That was the deal.

"I'm not asking my mom. I'm asking you."

He grunted something incoherent and started reading. My eyes tracked from the paper to his face, seeking any indication of what it said. I got nothing.

"Well? What does it say?" I inched forward to read it myself. He tilted the paper out of my view.

"You still planning on being Maddy?"

"What? What does that have to do with anything?"

"Answer the question. Are you still playing Maddy?"

I stared at Josh, tried to decipher the hatred behind his words. Josh and I had fought before, but this was different. This was intense. "Yeah, why?"

Josh shook his head and walked past me, stopping in front of my old locker. He smoothed the e-mail out and shoved it between the thin slots at the top.

I could get it out, but I'd have to open the locker. That hadn't gone so well my first day back, and I wasn't looking for a repeat performance of that spectacle. "What did you do that for?"

"Because *Maddy* didn't get in."

"Wait, you mean? Did they say no? They really said no?" I knew there was a chance, a strong possibility more likely, that I wouldn't get into RISD, but I had kind of refused to think about that, was banking on the yes until I had definitive proof otherwise. "Did you get in?"

I watched a smug grin play across his face. It made my stomach churn.

"Yeah, I did," he said. "Ella did, too, but there is no chance of me seeing her at RISD this fall, is there? So much for our plans."

Ella . . . *me* . . . I had gotten in. And he had, too. A huge grin covered my face, and it took every ounce of control I had not to throw my arms around him and cheer.

"What are you smiling for? You buried that dream with your lie."

No, I didn't. I never gave up on that dream. I put it on hold. For a little bit. Crap, he was right. "No. I'll fix this. I will."

"Umm hmm." Josh took a step closer, and I could

see the challenge in his eyes, the challenge for me to come clean. "And how, exactly, do you plan to do that, *Maddy*?"

Josh's head snapped up at the exact same time I felt two arms come around my waist. "Everything good here?" Alex asked.

Josh shrugged. "I don't know. Ask your girlfriend."

Alex's hands flexed on my stomach before he pulled me against his chest. I recognized it for what it was—a protective gesture. He dropped his head down to the crook of my neck and whispered, "You okay, baby?"

There was a threat in Alex's words, one not aimed at me, and for a brief second, I got a glimpse of what Maddy had seen in him. He always had her back. Always. I'd seen him toss a kid to the ground for looking at her funny, and I'd heard him chew out random girls in the cafeteria for commenting on something as ridiculous as her choice of shoes.

"I'm good," I said, letting myself draw strength from the warmth of his arms. "Bad morning, that's all."

"Yeah . . . bad morning," Josh replied. "Nothing more going on here than a bad morning."

Alex let me go and stepped out from behind me. I could see him struggling to stay calm as he spoke to Josh. "Did I miss something here?"

"Miss something? Yeah, you could say that," Josh said, and Alex tossed his hands out, silently asking Josh to explain. "Why didn't you tell me she asked to see me when she woke up?"

"She was out of it, Josh. She was upset and scared. She was having a hard enough time as it was making sense out of everything. The last thing she needed was to field your questions. I wasn't trying to hurt you, Josh. I was trying to keep her safe."

Josh took a step closer, tried his best to close the six-inch difference between him and his cousin. "That girl standing behind you took the one good thing I had. She took it without even thinking about what it would do to me, or her parents, or anyone else. And I want it back. I would've taken it that night if you'd done as she asked and called me."

I'd never seen them fight. I'd seen the two of them hurl mean comments at each other at family gatherings, but never once had I heard them actually fight. I started to speak, to beg Josh to stop talking and walk away, but Alex waved me off.

"There is absolutely nothing she can do to change things. Nothing," Alex said. "I've watched her cry herself to sleep trying to think of ways to make this better, Josh, but she can't. None of us can."

"You keep thinking that, Alex, and eventually maybe she'll start believing it, too."

Alex turned to look at me, confused as to what Josh was rattling on about. Josh had given me the perfect out, the perfect opportunity to come clean and walk away. I didn't take it. I pretended I had no idea what he was talking about.

Alex's entire demeanor softened. I don't know if he saw the fine tremor overtaking my body or if he realized exactly how broken Josh was, but he laid a gentle hand on Josh's shoulder and sighed. "I get what you have lost. I do. But she's already apologized, Josh. What more do you want from her?"

Josh shook his head, the anger I saw coursing through his eyes morphing into defeat. "I want nothing from her." He took a step sideways so he was looking squarely at me, speaking only to me. "But just because you apologized, doesn't mean I have to forgive you."

30

Alex waited until Josh was out of sight and our nosy classmates had gone back to their morning rituals before he grabbed my arm and towed me down the hall. There was a little alcove where an old water fountain used to be. He pushed me into it and scanned the hall to make sure no one was listening before he spoke.

"What's going on between you two?" There was no demand in his tone. It was nothing more than a simple question laced with confusion. I watched as his entire body went rigid, tense, almost like he didn't want me to answer, like he didn't want to know. In public, when our friends or Josh were listening, he'd be protective and kind, secure in where he stood with me. But here, in the relative privacy of this dark corner, he looked scared.

"Nothing is going on. He's upset about Ella. We both are. I was trying to help."

"I know he's the reason you left school early yesterday. You were talking to him in the staircase between classes and you went to his house last night."

"Are you following me?"

He actually looked offended that I would even suggest such a thing. "No, Maddy. I wasn't following you. I was here, fielding questions about your odd behavior, making up excuses about why you ran out of class and why you've decided to make Molly your new best friend. What I don't know is why you went to Josh's house instead of mine."

"I don't need you to make excuses for me," I said, irritated with myself for being too weak to handle one day in public as Maddy. "And Josh, well, I wouldn't worry about him, he's pretty much written me off."

"So you say." He was angry now, I could hear it in his tone as he struggled to keep his voice down and not make a scene. He leaned forward, and I felt his breath against my neck. "Because when my girlfriend leaves school without so much as a goodbye, doesn't answer her phone, and leaves another guy's house dressed in his clothes later that night . . . yeah, well, I kinda think I'm entitled to worry, wouldn't you say?"

How did he know I was wearing Josh's clothes? "Who told you that? Who told you where I was?"

He took a step back and braced his hand against the wall, giving himself enough space to calm down while keeping me from passing. "Doesn't matter who told me," he answered quietly. "I just want to know why. Why did you go to him instead of me? Why do you trust him more than me lately?"

Oh, it *did* matter who had told him. I managed to duck out from underneath his arm and scan the hall. It didn't take me long to find her, standing there pretending she was reading the notices on the student activities board. She wasn't reading crap. Besides, it's not like she had a life outside of stalking Josh. Kim had told him. That crazy girlfriend of Josh's had told him.

I didn't know who I was more upset with—Kim for sticking her nose where it didn't belong or Alex for actually thinking for a second Maddy would cheat on him. "You believe Kim? After everything, you believe her over me?"

"I wouldn't have two months ago. I wouldn't have two *days* ago. But since you came back to school—" He paused and shook his head. "*I* don't know you anymore, Maddy, and that scares the crap out of me."

"What's that supposed to mean?" I tried for angry, which wasn't a stretch considering I was fuming over Kim's meddling. "What are you trying to say?"

"First Molly, then Jenna, now Josh. Are you trying to lose everything?"

"So I am supposed to forget what happened, pretend I am happy, and go on like everything is perfect?"

"That's not what I meant, Maddy, and you know it. I'm the one person who actually gets what your sister meant to you. I remember every conversation we ever had about her, about how you wished you could be more confident like Ella and not care what people thought. How you wished you had half her talent. How you wished we had friends as loyal and honest as Josh."

I shook my head at his words, tears rimming my eyes. Maddy never wanted to be me; she'd said as much that night in the car. How she was tired of covering for me, tired of making excuses for my lack of social skills.

"You have no idea how much she meant to me. You couldn't," I said.

The anger and confusion I'd seen in Alex's eyes faded as he held out his hand to me. I took it and let him pull me in to his chest. "Josh may be able to tell you who your sister's favorite band was or how much salt she liked to dump on her pizza, but he can't remind you of the things you did when you were kids. He doesn't know about all the time you spent sitting on the hood of my car scanning the latest issue of the school's newspaper for her drawings."

I didn't know Maddy did that, didn't know she cared. "And you can? You can remind me of that?"

"Every day if that's what you need. You have told me so much about her, I can guarantee I know her as well as Josh does, maybe better."

"She applied to the Rhode Island School of Design, did you know that?"

Alex nodded. "Of course I did. You showed me the three drawings she was working on for her application."

The look on my face must have told him I had no

memory of that because he laughed before explaining. "The weekend before the accident we were at your house. We had stopped there on our way to Narragansett Beach because you wanted to change. Something about not having the right shoes on for the bonfire and sand. Ella was out with Josh. There was a modern art exhibit in Boston she wanted to see."

I remembered that day like it was yesterday. The exhibit was fantastic, but the two-hour ride to Boston sucked. That, and Kim had called every ten minutes asking when Josh would be home.

"I was complaining that we didn't have time to stop by your house *and* pick up the beer, but you insisted I come in, said it would only take a minute."

Nothing ever took Maddy a minute. "Sorry."

"Don't be. I'm not." Alex grinned, and I got the feeling they'd done a lot more than grab a different pair of shoes. "You went into her room to borrow her hairbrush and saw the application sitting on her desk with her sketches."

I'd actually shoved the application underneath a bunch of homework to keep Mom and Dad from seeing it. Maddy must have had to move a lot of stuff around to find it, but whatever. "Which one was your favorite?"

Alex dropped his backpack and pulled out his wallet, then handed me a folded piece of paper he had tucked inside. It was a photocopy of a picture I drew of Maddy freshman year. We were about a month into school and the sting of her no longer wanting to be seen with me was still raw. I used to sit at the table and sketch while Josh and his friends talked. I'd draw everything from the trash can to the clock on the wall, but this one was of Maddy. It was crude—sucked, actually—but it was definitely her. And it wasn't one I even had in the pile of contenders for my art school portfolio.

"I know where she kept the real one," I said. "You can have it if you want."

"No. You keep it," Alex said as he took his copy back.

"She got in to RISD. That's what I was talking to Josh about. They were planning on going together. That's why he was so upset."

"Did you think she wouldn't get in?" Alex asked. "She was amazing, Maddy. Better than Josh."

"I don't know what to think anymore. I don't know how to make any of this right."

He shook his head, his words coming after a long sigh. "There is nothing to make right, Maddy. The roads were wet and you weren't going that fast. I was there when you woke up, when the police questioned you. You weren't drunk. They gave you two blood alcohol tests and both of them showed nothing. It's been ruled an accident. What happened to your sister *was* an accident."

"I know that." I was mumbling, could hear the sad desperation in my voice. "But things are different now. I'm different now. The Maddy before the accident . . . it's like I don't know her anymore. I don't know what to say or how I am supposed to act."

It felt good to finally admit it, to acknowledge that I was as confused as he was. "Everything was easier then," I whispered. "I want to go back to that night and start over, trade places with her."

"You mean you wish you had died instead of her?" Alex asked. I didn't expect the flash of pain I heard in Alex's voice, didn't expect him to shrink away from me.

"Yes. No. Maybe. I don't know anymore. I'm tired of pretending. I'm tired of trying to be someone I am not." It was the first honest thing I'd said to him, and it felt good, fantastic even, for once, to be myself.

"You mean you want to be like her? Like Ella?" Alex asked as he pulled me into his arms and guided my head to his chest.

"Maybe I do. Maybe I want to be exactly like Ella," I whispered.

"That's not who you are, Maddy."

That's exactly who I am, I said silently to myself.

"Remember when you first learned what happened to Molly? Remember how hard that was?"

I thought back to last year, tried to connect Maddy to Molly's social downfall, but I got nothing. If anything, Maddy was her normal, I-don't-have-time-for-you self. When she wasn't home or at school, she was wherever Alex was. But that wasn't unusual; since freshman year, since the day she first sat down at his table, they'd been inseparable.

"And?" I didn't know what else to say and that seemed like the vaguest way to keep him talking.

"It got better. After a few months, people stopped gossiping about her. You stopped worrying so much that people would figure out what you'd done and things went back to normal. In time, this will get better, too."

"Time," I repeated. It seemed like such a simple solution. Such an insanely logical and completely stupid solution.

Alex reached down and picked up the backpack I'd dropped and looped it over his own shoulder. "Just be yourself—the you of the last three years, and I promise you, everything will be fine."

31

Being the old Maddy wasn't as hard as I thought.
With Alex thinking I was two steps away from losing it, he made running interference his full-time job, deflecting any question that came my way. He opted out of lunch in the cafeteria and let me retreat to the library where no one would bother me. Although I think that was more about keeping me away from Molly and Josh than my mental stability. The reason didn't matter; it worked the same.

I kept my distance from Josh for the rest of the day. It helped that he and Maddy weren't in any of the same classes. I caught him glancing my way in the hall the following afternoon, but Alex quickly moved in, blocking my view and distracting me. I didn't catch what he was saying, just the words *Snow Ball* and *colors.*

I quickly looked up at the posters covering the walls.

Some were advertising ticket sales and others were promoting Jenna for Snow Ball queen. They all had some combination of pink and purple in them so it seemed like a safe guess. "Pink, I think, maybe purple," I said, then went back to sorting books in my locker.

"You want me to wear a purple tie?"

"What?"

He took the few books I had in my hand and shoved them into my bag. "I asked if you expected me to wear a purple tie."

I shook my head, trying uselessly to understand why the color of his tie mattered. He could wear a black-and-orange-striped one for all I cared. "Uh . . . no," I said, hoping that was the correct response. "Wear a black one or a blue one. Either one is fine; I don't care."

"Well, what color is your dress?"

"What dress?" The closest I'd come to wearing a dress in the last ten years was an overly long shirt, and even then, I threw on a pair of wool leggings.

"The one you bought with Jenna way back in September."

I mentally shuffled through Maddy's closet. She had at least a dozen formal dresses in there. I'd gone through her entire closet the past three days, trying everything on in an attempt to make myself look exactly like her. But I hadn't seen any dresses with tags or still wrapped in plastic. "I don't know. Brown?"

"Really, brown?" Alex looked surprised and grunted in disgust.

I immediately understood my mistake. Outside of a pair of gloves and a scarf, Maddy didn't own a single article of clothing that was brown. Nothing even tan. Crap. "Doesn't matter, I wasn't planning on going."

"Uh, yeah, you are."

"No, I'm not." The last dance I went to was our father-daughter dance in elementary school. Dad had to split his time between Maddy and me. Half an hour in, I gave up, let Maddy monopolize his time while I played mat ball with the boys in the gym. "Why does it matter if I go, anyway? You go."

"I am going. With you."

I shook my head. I wasn't budging on this one. It was one thing to be Maddy at school where I could escape to the bathroom or the library to regain my sanity. It was something completely different to be put on display, to have to walk in heels and make small talk about who was wearing what, or more accurately, who was doing who. It was only a matter of time before Jenna, Alex, and this entire school figured out what Josh already had—I was no Maddy Lawton.

"You are the one who told me to avoid Josh and Molly. I think *not* going is the perfect idea," I told Alex.

He laughed and started walking away, then turned around when he was a few feet from me and held out his hand. Apparently, I was supposed to follow. "Last I checked, Josh wasn't going," he said. "And I doubt Molly will go without a date, so you are good there, too."

I couldn't help the sudden joy that filled me. I knew Kim wanted to go; she'd been talking about it since they started dating. How cool it was going to be to go to the Snow Ball with a senior. She went so far as to try to set me up with someone, figuring I could double with them. I didn't have to put a stop to that; Josh did it for me, warning her that setting me up was nearly as horrible an idea as him going to the dance in the first place. I'd assumed by now she had worn him down.

"Josh isn't going?"

Alex gave me a cursory glance, no doubt wondering why I cared. "Last I checked, he doesn't do much of anything. Since the night of the accident, I've seen him at school and at your sister's burial service but that's it. Outside of school, he is a virtual shut-in."

I yanked Alex to a stop and pulled my hand free. "Wait. Him and Kim."

Alex shook his head. "How should I know? And besides, why do you care?"

"I don't," I said, hoping he'd believe me. "It would suck if he didn't go because of—"

"Don't worry about him. He needs some time, Maddy. Everyone does."

———

Alex threaded his fingers through mine and tugged me the few remaining feet to the girls' locker room. He knocked once before opening the door a crack and yelled in to see if it was empty. School had ended over a half hour ago. Anybody still in there was going to get chewed out for being late for practice.

When no one answered, he pushed the door all the way open and peeked inside. Seeing nothing, he pulled me in. "I figured you hadn't seen this yet."

With the exception of gym, which my broken wrist had blessedly excused me from, I never set foot in the girls' locker room. I didn't play a sport and saw no need to shower at school. But I knew exactly where Maddy's locker was. There was an entire block of them set aside for the field hockey team. Maddy's was smack in the middle, her name artfully etched into the metal.

Tucked in the corner of the locker room was a roll of paper, not unlike the ones Josh and I used when we were sketching out murals. Alex handed me the edge and motioned for me to lay it flat on the floor. I did, using one of the field hockey sticks sitting on the bench to anchor it.

It was huge, easily spanning the length of seven lockers. WELCOME BACK, MADDY. Names of people I didn't know covered the entire surface. Alex's was there, Jenna's, too. Keith, Molly, Hannah, and a couple of other kids I recognized from Maddy's lunch table. The rest . . .

I gave up trying to place faces with the names and started counting. Seventy-three total.

"They're planning on hanging this at the field hockey game this Friday," Alex said as he held the other side down with his hand. "To celebrate your first week back at school."

I read a few of the notes, glancing over most. Alex's message was tagged with an *I love you*, and Jenna had scribbled out a curt *Get well soon*. Molly's was the longest. She'd wished me well like the rest of them, but also written an offer of help, her pretty handwriting saying she'd be there to listen if I needed someone to talk to. Funny how the one person Alex had warned me to steer clear of was the one person who had offered to help.

"That's why you are going," Alex said, cutting into my thoughts. "Jenna may be pushing hard for Snow Ball queen, but she won't win. I made sure of that. And, well, no one is running against me for king, so . . ."

I turned and stared at him. I'd pegged him completely wrong. I had expected him to be egocentric and obsessed with popularity. But at the end of the day, no matter how obsessed he seemed to be with his image, he cared more about Maddy.

"I have been back at school for three days, Alex. Three short days. I'm not ready yet." And seeing well wishes sprawled across the banner didn't help. If anything, it made it worse, kicked the expectations up a notch.

"I know," he said. "But it's only November. You have a couple more weeks to figure things out. Besides, it's not like you have a choice, and it's not like you'll be alone. I'll be there to help you. Our friends will, too."

32

It was past six when I got home. I expected Mom to be worried, maybe angry. I hadn't talked to her since Monday when I ran out and left her crying on her bedroom floor.

The house was dark and the driveway was empty except for Mom's SUV. I opened the front door and was greeted by the dog. No smell of dinner cooking, no TV blaring the news. Only darkness surrounded by silence.

I flipped on a light and dropped my backpack to the floor. The kitchen looked exactly the same as this morning—coffeepot still filled with sludge, dishes still in the sink, dog still covered with day-old soup. I turned off the coffee, dumped the grounds into the trash, and gave Bailey a quick paper towel and water bath. I thought about doing the dishes, but the dishwasher was full *and* clean. That meant I'd have to empty it first, which I didn't want to do.

"Mom," I called, but I got no answer. I wondered if she was out with Dad. Maybe she had gone with him to pick up dinner or something.

Turning on lights as I went, I made my way upstairs. Bailey had made it up ahead of me and was lying on my old bed. I stopped and stared at him, waited for him to jump down and come to me. He didn't budge, didn't so much as lift his head to acknowledge my presence. My own dog was turning on me.

With a silent vow to feed him nothing more than dry food until he changed his attitude, I turned around and headed for Maddy's room. I had to find a brown dress somewhere in her closet or find the time to buy one in the next few weeks. Alex wasn't letting me out of going to the dance, and until I came up with an amazing reason why I couldn't go, I had to play along.

There was a flicker of light coming from underneath my parents' door. I listened for a moment before pushing it open. Mom was there, sound asleep in the overstuffed chair in the corner. The TV was muted. She'd showered— her hair was damp, her face free of makeup, and she was already in her pajamas. I watched her for a minute. I hadn't seen her this quiet or this peaceful in weeks, and I wondered if it was sheer exhaustion or the help of a few sleeping pills that had stilled her mind.

She had my old baby blanket tucked around her, and I couldn't help but walk over and touch it, let the tattered softness calm me as well. I saw a cell phone in her hand. I quickly pulled mine out of my pocket and searched through the call list. Alex, Dad, and Alex again. Nothing from Mom. Nothing from Josh.

I carefully took the phone from her hand and dialed the last number she called. It was mine . . . Ella's. It went to voice mail, my less-than-enthusiastic directions telling whoever was looking for me to leave a message. From the call log on Mom's phone, she'd dialed my number fifteen times in the last day, probably so she could hear the distant echo of my voice.

"I'm sorry," I whispered before I laid the phone on the floor beside her and left the room. Waking her now was pointless. I wasn't ready to deal with her tears.

I was pretty familiar with Maddy's closet by now, knew she kept shirts on the left-hand side, organized by season, then color. Jeans hung in the middle followed by skirts and dresses. Her shoes and boots were in their original boxes stacked neatly in the back. And on the far right, tucked behind her jackets, were her formal gowns.

I started there, sorted through three short black dresses, one long shiny-looking red thing, and a top that I would barely classify as a shirt before I found something that would work. It was a dark cream, not brown or tan, but I figured muddy cream was in the same color spectrum so I could talk my way out of that minor discrepancy.

Shoes were a different story. The dress wasn't new, so I figured whatever shoes she'd bought to go with it would be at the back of the stack. Maddy was never one for recycling clothing. I sat down cross-legged in front of her closet and started sorting through boxes. Red heels, black sparkly flats, some sort of wedge-sandal-type thing. None of them would work. I needed cream shoes, or so I thought. Honestly, I would be fine wearing flip-flops.

I pulled out another box, totally expecting to find an expensive pair of the-wrong-color heels wrapped in tissue paper. I opened the lid, reached in, and came up not with a shoe but a stack of paper. I recognized the first sheet—it was a picture I'd drawn a few years ago, back while we were in middle school. Nothing but a simple rose, its thorny stem weaving around the finger of an anonymous hand. Beneath that was a birthday card I'd given Maddy last year. She hadn't given me mine until three days later. She said she'd forgotten it at school or something like that. She had every test I'd ever taken for her, copies of the art awards I'd won, and twelve years' worth of school pictures tucked into that one shoe box.

For as many papers and pictures as I pulled out, I didn't find one thing that was hers. Not a note, a report card, a class picture, nothing that referenced her. This box was about me.

Wondering how long she had been keeping a box of my mementos, I dug through the papers, figuring the oldest things would be at the bottom of the pile. The last paper was thin, not enough weight to be a photo or another one of my drawings. Afraid that it would tear, I pulled it out and carefully unfolded it. It was an article from the local newspaper about Cranston High's field hockey team. It was dated the day after they lost divisionals. According to the article, the reason they lost was simple—Molly Crahan, one of the best goalies in the state, hadn't played.

Tossing the box aside, I continued reading. The article didn't say why she hadn't played. It made no mention of her testing positive for drugs the day before or the school suspending her from the team for the remainder of the season. The reporter did say, however, that had Molly played, Cranston High School would've won. A few lines down, the details got too real . . . too close to home. Maddy had highlighted her own name, underlined every reference to the three shoot-outs she had lost, but left any mention of her nine saves untouched.

I moved to the bed and dumped the rest of the box out, pushing aside everything that related to me until I was left with a pile of things related to Molly. There was a blurb from the newspaper's police log indicating that they had broken up a party at Alex's house two nights before divisionals, citing a noise violation, and a letter from the athletic director explaining the disciplinary actions taken against a member of the field hockey team for failing a random drug test. Behind that was a picture of my sister and Molly, one I think she had clipped out of a yearbook. It was them in their sophomore year, at the first field hockey game they'd played together at the varsity level.

I froze when I found a bag of pills, wondering why my sister had them. She had passed the drug test the day before divisionals. That one and every other one the school had randomly subjected them to since.

I emptied the bag of pills onto the bed, counting three. These didn't come out of a bottle you could get at any drugstore. They were different, powdery and white, not a single identifying mark on them. And they were hidden in Maddy's closet in the bottom of a shoe box.

I put them back in the bag and shoved them under the mattress. I should've flushed them. I wanted to flush them, but something forced me to hang on to them.

There were a few more pictures of Molly in the pile and a copy of this year's team roster. Molly was on it, but her name was at the end of the list. She'd made the team this year, but I doubted she'd play.

Near the bottom of the pile was an index card with an address for the Lighthouse Clinic and a room number.

That name sounded vaguely familiar, and I quickly Googled it on my phone. What came up had my eyes growing wide as my mind spun in circles. It was a hospital, a drug treatment center for teens, to be exact. In an instant,

I knew why Maddy had it and who had been a patient there—Molly.

I remembered the day she went. I'd overheard my parents telling Maddy why Molly would be out of school for a few weeks. Molly was still claiming she hadn't taken anything, but the school had two positive test results showing otherwise. Mom wanted to know if anybody else on the team was using drugs. Dad wanted to know if Maddy had *ever* taken anything. I clearly remembered Maddy denying everything. *Everything.*

I sifted through the scraps of paper on the bed, trying to figure out why my sister was keeping bits and pieces of information on a person she'd essentially shunned. There wasn't a personal note in there. Aside from the clinic's handwritten address, everything she had collected was official—letters from the school about the incident, newspaper clippings, photos. Nothing gave me a clue about why Maddy seemed to have been secretly obsessed with Molly.

Every shoe box in the closet got opened, every drawer in her desk was torn apart, each of her ten unused purses was searched, but I found nothing. Not a ribbon-tied stack of letters from Alex. Not a scrapbook of Maddy's own accomplishments. Nothing but that shoe box outlining my life and Molly's demise.

I tossed everything related to me back into the box and neatly stacked the papers referencing Molly into one pile, then shoved it under the mattress where the pills were. I no longer cared about the last two field hockey games of the season, or the dance, or how I was going to lie my way out of going to either. I was concerned with one thing—finding out what Maddy had done to Molly and why.

33

As far as I could tell, Dad hadn't come home last night. His car wasn't in the driveway, and the coffee cup he always used was still sitting in the cabinet. I let myself believe he was traveling; that was better than contemplating the obvious.

Before leaving, I turned the coffeepot on for Mom and laid out her cup. I didn't want her to think that nobody had come home, that nobody cared. I did, I just didn't know how to tell her.

I skipped my first period class and parked myself outside the door of Josh's AP Physics class. He was beyond upset with me, and I didn't deserve his help, but I didn't know who else to turn to. If anyone could help me figure out what was going on, it was him. And if he couldn't, then at least he'd listen to me.

I could hear Mr. Walden asking questions about potential energy, electric potential, and electric potential difference. I didn't know the answers. Less than a month of being Maddy, and I was already losing intellectual ground. Bonus was, I'd figured out how to curl my lashes. Who needed to understand what a joule was when you could do that?

The bell rang, and I stood up, watching and waiting for Josh to walk out.

"Hey," I said, and reached out to stop him. He'd seen me and was planning on ignoring me. "I need to talk to you."

"You get Alex's approval for that?" he asked.

"I don't need Alex's permission."

Josh laughed and walked past me. I hurried to catch up with him. He was my best friend, and I deserved his anger for what I'd done, his hatred even, but I didn't want to lose him.

"Stop," I yelled. Everyone in the hallway, including Josh, swung their heads in my direction. I gave them a mind-your-own-business stare, then quickly caught up to Josh. "I need your help."

I could see the elation in his eyes as he took a step closer and bent down to whisper into my ear. He laced his fingers through mine and pulled me aside, at least giving us the appearance of privacy. "Okay, I think we should start with your parents. They can help us figure out how to tell Alex and everybody else. I know you're worried that they will—"

I pulled my hand free and took a step back. "Wait, what?"

"I mean, sure they're going to be surprised and confused, but I don't think they'll hate you if that's what you are worried about. They love you."

"I'm not telling them who I am, Josh."

"Okay, I get that. So we can tell somebody else first, maybe my mom. She can help us figure out what to say to your parents, probably be there when you tell them if that's what you want."

"No, you don't get it. I'm not telling them. Ever. Maddy deserved to live. That's what I'm doing, making sure she does."

He shrank back at my words as if he'd been slapped. "But you said you needed my help."

"I do, but not with that. With something Maddy did . . . or something I think she did, anyway. I know why she hung out with Jenna now, why she put up with her crap." And it had nothing to do with Maddy feeling bad for Jenna and her family situation. My guess was, Jenna knew exactly what had happened to Molly, that somehow my sister was involved and Jenna was holding it over Maddy's head, using it to slowly take everything important away from her.

I stood there and watched his faith in me disappear, his optimism deflating as my true intentions finally took form. "You're still going to be her? You still *want* to be her?"

What I wanted had nothing to do with it, but that didn't change my answer. "Yes."

232

He shook his head and backed up, put what felt like miles of distance between us. "Then I can't help you. In fact, as far as I'm concerned, I don't know you anymore."

He walked away from me. No *I understand.* No *If you change your mind, I'll be here.* Not even an *It will be okay, we'll figure it out.* Nothing more than a clearly delivered, soul-crushing *I don't want you in my life anymore.*

"Did you mean what you said last night? Before you left?" I called after him.

Slowly, Josh turned around, his anger still firmly in place. "Did I love Ella? Is that what you are asking me?"

I nodded, quite aware that every word I spoke was being uploaded to YouTube or texted across the entire school.

"I meant it. I have since the day I met her. Still do."

"Then why didn't you ever tell her? You spent nearly every second of every day together and you never thought to tell her? Never thought she'd want to know or that per-haps she felt the same way?"

He took a step toward me, then stopped. His hands tensed at his sides, his tone low, guttural as if he was fighting to speak through his gritted teeth. "She was never, *ever*, on her own. And as for why I didn't tell her . . . well, she never seemed ready to hear it. Still doesn't."

34

I couldn't move, couldn't even muster the resolve to look around me. It took an enormous amount of effort just to stay upright, not to dissolve in a pile of tears in the middle of the hall.

"Trouble with your sister's boyfriend?" I swung my head around at the sound of her voice, wondered exactly how long Jenna had been standing there and how much she'd heard.

"Piece of advice," she said. "Try worrying less about your dead sister and more about yourself."

It was no secret that Jenna had had no use for Ella. She'd made that clear at the party the night my sister died. Part of me hoped it was a façade, something she did in public to keep up her image. To hear her express it in private, to me, wounded me in a way I wouldn't have thought possible.

"What is that supposed to mean?"

"Oh, please, Maddy. Are you blind? Have you looked in the mirror lately? You look like crap, and your behavior kind of reminds me a bit of Molly's. You want to be her? The fragile girl who everyone thinks is crazy?"

"Are you kidding me, Jenna? Do you have any idea what she—"

Jenna cut me off with a wave of her hand, the sarcastic grin spreading across her face too telling. "Oh, I know exactly what she went through. But they let her back on the team this year, so I guess all is forgiven."

I was confused as to why Jenna found this amusing. Her reaction, frankly, was downright twisted. I didn't care about pretending to be Maddy in that moment, didn't care if I slipped up and she figured out who I really was. I wasn't going to spend the rest of the year being her friend. Forget Alex and his you-have-to-play-nice-with-Jenna attitude. I was done with her.

"I don't get you. For the life of me, I can't figure out why we are even friends."

"Because we're exactly the same," Jenna replied.

I shook my head. I refused to believe that. The Maddy I'd shared a room with for the first ten years of my life, the Maddy Mom and Dad adored, the one who still made cards for our grandmother at Christmas could never be as cruel and self-serving as Jenna.

"Deny it if you want," Jenna continued. "You and I both know it's the truth."

"No. It's not." I don't know where my courage came from, but I didn't care. I had waited three long years to tell Jenna what I thought of her, and I wasn't going to stop myself now. "I am nothing like you. I don't use my family problems as an excuse to treat everybody like crap, and I would never go crying to my best friend's boyfriend about how mean my father is or how broke we are. You think crying to Alex is going to gain you sympathy points, gonna make him dump me to take care of you?"

Jenna reached over and grabbed my arm, towed me into the girls' bathroom across the hall. She kicked open each stall to make sure they were all empty before turning to the two girls staring at us from the sink. "Get out," she yelled. "Now!"

She slammed the door shut behind them and put her ear to the wood—I presumed to make sure no one was eavesdropping. I didn't know how she could tell, but I guessed certain types of people, those who are well versed in gossipy behavior, had their ways.

"You have shut me out for nearly a month, letting Alex be your go-between. I don't know why, and, to be honest, I don't care because it's absolutely working in my favor."

"In your favor? How is my accident working in your favor?"

"Alex loves you. I'll give you that. But he'll only put up with this"—arms fluttered in my direction—"for so long."

I didn't try to keep the contempt from my voice. I embraced it and let my words come out in a low growl. "Put up with what?"

"Oh, come on. Did you hit your head that hard?"

I toyed with actually answering her. I had hit the tree hard enough that I had no freaking clue who I was when I woke up. It took staring at my cold, dead sister in the hospital morgue to jar my memory. So yeah . . . kinda.

"For the first couple of days, I thought you were upset, you know . . . torn up about your sister and feeling guilty, but you had Alex answering my texts and returning my calls." She paused long enough to laugh. "But you have even shut him out completely."

"That's not true," I fired back. She had no idea what Alex and I had talked about when he was at my house, no idea how many times he sat there quietly holding my hand when I refused to talk. I hadn't shut Alex out. The only person I was keeping on the outside was Jenna, and that was purposeful.

"It's true, and you know it. If you pulled yourself out of your own pity party for half a second, you'd see it."

I'd killed my own sister; I think that alone entitled me to a bit of self-inflicted guilt. But that wasn't what had me broken and stumbling through the motions of being Maddy. She wasn't *merely* my sister. She was a part of me, the one person I knew would always be there. And now she was gone. I missed her, and no matter what lie I told or how much time passed, I couldn't get the overwhelming feeling of complete emptiness to go away.

"So what if I was a little distant. It's to be expected given what I've been through." I knew for a fact nobody would think twice about me being quiet, more reserved than the Maddy they knew. In fact, the one time Mom had brought it up to my doctors they told her it was normal, that anger and refusal to talk were normal stages of the grieving process.

"There is a difference between being quiet and completely freezing someone out, Maddy. When was the last time you and Alex slept together?"

I was genuinely confused. I didn't know the answer to that, couldn't hazard a guess. He'd tried that night in my room, but I'd pushed him away, not wanting to go there.

"You can't even remember, can you?" she continued when I didn't answer. "When was the last time you were on a date with him or let him kiss you? Not coddle you, but actually kiss you."

"That's none of your business."

"He's not forty, Maddy. And you sure as hell aren't married. He's eighteen. He has absolutely no reason to stick by you." She eased forward over the sink and adjusted her hair in the mirror. "And there are plenty of others more than willing to take your place."

"And by others, you mean you."

Jenna turned around and grinned. "I didn't say that." She didn't exactly *not* say it either. "But I have come to a decision about something else."

"And that is?"

"I want to be the Snow Ball queen. You had your turn last year. Now it's mine."

I couldn't care less about the Snow Ball or that ninety-nine-cent crown Jenna was after. As far as I was concerned, Jenna could have every one of the plastic crowns hanging from Maddy's mirror. I'd box them up and give them to her tonight if that's what she wanted.

"Last I checked, voting ends tomorrow. Maybe you should step up your game," I said. I might not have been interested in her popularity contest, but there was no way I was going to let her know that.

"Nope. You're going to find a way to back out. I don't care what you say or what lie you come up with, just do it."

"And if I don't?"

She leaned in as if afraid somebody in this completely empty bathroom would hear us. "You think Alex loves you enough to go to jail for you? He's got a full scholarship to Syracuse to play soccer. You think he's going to risk that to defend you?"

"Alex didn't do anything!" I yelled. Or at least I thought he hadn't.

"He knew what you were planning to do and covered it up for you afterward. Always protecting his precious Maddy. The way I see it, that makes him as guilty as you. So yeah, you'll do as I say, because if you don't, I'll bury you, then him."

35

The thin newspaper clipping in my back pocket was like a dead weight that slowed me down and consumed my thoughts. I'd done nothing but think about what it meant. I wondered how I was going to figure it out without Josh, and I was curious as to whether Jenna's threat had anything to do with it.

I walked into the cafeteria. Everyone was sitting in their usual spots—Alex on top of the table, Jenna to his left vying for attention. Molly was at the end, three empty seats between her and the rest of Maddy's friends. She had her Physics book out, a pencil in her hand and a notebook open next to it, seeming completely uninterested in the conversations going on around her.

Alex saw me and hopped down, waving me over. I should've walked over to him, sat down in my assigned seat, and pretended to be interested in whatever he and

Jenna were talking about. But Molly looked so distant, so removed from everyone around her.

"Hey, why are you sitting by yourself?" I'd always wondered why she never tried to make new friends, why nobody, including Josh and me, never once thought to include her.

She looked up from her book, her eyes drifting to Alex before settling back on me. "It's easier. I tried to make other friends, but eventually they had questions that I didn't want to answer. Besides, I don't mind sitting by myself so much anymore."

I pulled out the chair across from her and sat down. She reminded me of myself those first few days of school after Maddy had made her friends and I was still fumbling my way around. And right now, I could use a little dose of me.

"You know they are both staring at you," Molly whispered to me.

"Who?" I asked, pretty sure I could guess.

"Alex and Josh. They've been watching you ever since you sat down here with me."

I was almost positive Josh had been watching me for longer than that. I'd caught him looking at me when I walked in. He'd held my gaze for a second before shaking his head in disgust and turning back to Kim. Alex, well . . . he didn't want me talking to Molly.

I leaned in, hoping Alex wouldn't hear my hushed words. "Alex is a bit overprotective these days," I explained.

"And Josh, well, he was close to Ella, so he blames me for a whole bunch of things."

"I'd like to say that things get easier, that after a while people will stop treating you like damaged goods. But as you can see," she said, gesturing toward herself, "that's not the case."

She giggled at her last words, and I joined in, happy to hear the brutal honesty that everyone else was afraid to give me. "Yeah, well, I don't mind being ignored. Kind of a nice change of pace."

"Ignored, huh? I guess that's one way to put it." She went back to her homework, her attention shifting every so often to me. I guess she thought I was going to leave, that I'd get up and take my normal seat by Alex. Little did she know, I liked it next to her. I was comfortable there.

She flipped the page and gnawed on the top of her mechanical pencil as she mouthed the words to the next problem. I watched as she worked it out, erasing and re-writing the equation three times.

"You're doing it wrong," I said, and reached for her notebook. I copied the problem on a clean line, then solved it, making sure to show my calculations so she could see how I'd done it.

"It's easy," I said as I nudged the notebook back in her direction. "You gotta follow the same steps every time."

She looked at my answer, then flipped to the back of the book to make sure it was correct. "How did you do that? I mean, you're failing Physics."

"Was," I corrected. As far as I was concerned, Maddy was never failing another class again. "And besides, I'm not as dumb as everyone thinks."

"Nobody thinks you're dumb," Alex said as he reached around me and yanked the notebook from Molly's hands.

"The answer is right," Molly said. "I already checked it."

Alex glanced at the problem, then at me as if trying to figure out how I'd done it. Muttering something under his breath, he tossed the notebook onto the table. I swear I caught a glint of suspicion in his eyes, one that had me simultaneously filled with hope and fear—hope that he'd realize who I was and let me out of the confines of my lie, and fear of the rain of crap that was going to pour down on me if he did.

"Ella was helping me," I quickly said, praying that he'd buy my excuse. "If I fail Physics, I'll get kicked off the field hockey team, so she was tutoring me at home, teaching me how to do it."

"You could've asked me," Alex said. "I would've helped you."

I'd forgotten he was a decent student and could pull a B in the regular college prep course without too much effort. He could've helped Maddy, and I found it odd that she hadn't ever asked him to. Instead, she always came to me to bail her out.

"I could've done a lot of things differently," I said.

36

Dad was sitting at the kitchen table when I got home, his entire focus on the small cup of coffee he had in front of him. He looked up when he heard me come in and tried for a smile, but it was small and filled with exhaustion. Wherever he was last night, it was obvious he hadn't slept.

"Hey," I said. "When did you get home?"

"Couple of hours ago," he replied. "I had some things to catch up on at work, then I went to your grandmother's for dinner."

I'd assumed he'd gone there . . . was hoping he'd gone there, but the confirmation was still nice.

"Your grandmother sends her love," Dad said as he pushed the spoon around his coffee. "I wanted to bring you with me. I thought maybe some time away from school and this house would do you good."

We had spent a lot of time at my grandmother's growing up. She used to let us eat our dessert before dinner and never worried about the amount of dirt we tracked into the house. Even as a teenager I loved going there, loved the way she doted on me and made my favorite foods.

She used to draw like me, except she was better. She could paint, too. I never seemed to be able to master that—the whole color thing. I still preferred my charcoal pencils to acrylics and oils. It was my grandmother who gave Maddy and me our first sketchbooks. They were actually old ones of hers that she'd tossed aside. Didn't matter. To us, they were massive sheets of clean paper that we wouldn't get in trouble for writing on.

"I texted you a few times, but you didn't respond," Dad said.

I pulled out my phone and scrolled through my texts. There were three from Dad. I remembered my phone chiming in Spanish class. The teacher gave me a stern glare, and I'd turned it off without checking to see who the text was from. I had no idea it was Dad or I would've responded.

"Sorry," I said, and shoved my phone back into my pocket. "I talked to Josh like you suggested."

"You find the answers you were looking for?"

"No," I said. "Just a lot more questions."

"Any of those questions I can help answer?"

I took a seat across from him and grabbed an orange

from the fruit bowl in the center of the table. I wasn't hungry, but I peeled it anyway. "No."

"Well, I'm here if you're looking for someone to talk to."

"Thanks."

We sat there in silence—Dad hyperfocused on his coffee, and me on the lack of activity in the house. It was quiet, too quiet. Even Bailey was penned up in his crate, his nose pressed against the door.

"Can I let him out?" I asked, wondering what he'd done to earn time in jail.

Dad shrugged. "Sure, but he's only going to pace a circle in Ella's room and whine. It gets irritating after a while."

I unclicked the latch and tapped my hand against the side of my leg. Bailey edged his way out, his eyes on Dad as if he was waiting to be scolded or locked back up. When Dad stayed silent, Bailey came to me and lay down on my feet.

"Where's Mom?" I asked. She was the one I was used to seeing when I came home from school.

"Upstairs reading."

I didn't ask what she was reading. I didn't need to. The way his voice dropped off to nothing more than a pained whisper was answer enough. She was reading our journals, the ones I saw in her room the other day, the ones Maddy and I kept as kids.

"She seems different now, sadder than before. It's been nearly a month since . . ." I trailed off, unwilling to say the actual words. "Why does she seem more upset now?"

"Because you returned to school."

Confused as to why that mattered, I said, "But I've always gone to school. Me going back—that was always the plan."

"The entire time you were in the hospital, she was there, talking to the doctors and keeping you company. Then when you were home, she had you to take care of. Doctor's appointments, prescriptions, watching you, making sure you were comfortable. Now that you're back at school, she has nothing but her own thoughts to occupy her mind. And right now, well, those thoughts aren't good."

I was only home for a little over a week, but Mom spent every one of them hovering over me, asking me what I wanted to eat, kicking Alex out so I could rest, and talking to the teachers about the work I'd missed. It had bothered me back then. I figured her constant prodding was to keep me from losing it, from slipping into the darkness of my own mind. Little did I know, she was doing it to keep herself sane.

"I could stay home tonight if you want."

Dad shook his head and stood up, poured his full cup of coffee into the sink. "No. Go and be with your friends. Go out with Alex. Don't worry, I'll be here. I'll get her through this."

I didn't want to go, not when I was the one who had put her here, in a hell she couldn't seem to escape. A dark pit of my own making.

"Do you think we will be okay?"

Dad tensed, his hands braced on the edges of the sink. I heard every tick of the clock on the wall, felt every beat of my heart hammering in my head as I waited for him to turn around and answer. When he finally did, I could see the worry etched on his face, the confident, it-will-all-be-okay attitude I'd come to depend on stripped away, replaced with an uncertainty that had me terrified.

"I will make sure *you* are okay, Maddy. I promise you that."

"That's not what I asked."

I watched as he weighed his next words, his mouth opening on a sigh before he finally spoke. "I don't know, Maddy. She's hurting, and there is nothing I can do to fix it. Nothing any of us can do."

I got up to leave the kitchen, his last words thundering around my mind. Mom was in so much pain—pain I had caused and couldn't fix. And seeing Dad sitting there, worrying about everyone and everything, made things worse, made the guilt I was carrying around that much heavier.

"Maddy?" Dad whispered after me. I stopped, but didn't turn around. "I meant what I said the other day. I never once imagined what it would be like if your sister had lived instead of you. I loved . . . *love* you both more than my own life. Your mother does, too."

37

Alex had soccer practice. I wasn't sure what time it ended or what field he was playing on, so I parked next to his car in the lot and waited. It wasn't like I had anything better to do. I was pretty sure Dad wanted time alone to talk with Mom, and Josh didn't want anything to do with me. It was either sit here and wait for Alex or drive around aimlessly for hours.

I flipped the light on in my car and pulled the newspaper clipping from my back pocket. The words hadn't changed since I'd read it last. No new clues hidden between the lines, no explanations waiting to be discovered. Same smudged ink hiding a secret.

The sound of voices broke into my thoughts. I looked up and saw the entire soccer team walking toward the lot. Some still had their practice uniforms on, but most had changed, their cleats dangling from their hands.

It took me a few minutes to spot Alex. He was near the center of the group, arguing with the kid walking next to him. Alex shifted his weight as if hoisting something farther up his back. It wasn't until he spun around that I realized what—no, *who* he was carrying. Jenna.

He dropped her the second he saw me. She stumbled to her feet cursing but kept her arms around his neck. Her head tilted as she whispered something in his ear. It wasn't until Alex pointed out my car that she backed away from him, that flirty grin of hers transforming to a pout. She didn't bother to say hello to me as she passed my car, rather gave me a thanks-a-lot glare.

Alex opened my car door and slid into the passenger seat, tossing his gear bag into the back. "Everything okay? What are you doing here?"

I waved my hand in Jenna's direction. "What is *she* doing here?"

"Field hockey practice, Maddy. The semifinals are to-morrow. You know that. You were supposed to be there."

I looked out the windshield. Maddy's teammates were there, hanging on one soccer player or another, but that didn't make me feel better about Jenna plastering herself to Alex.

"The coach will give you a free pass this week. I had Jenna talk to him, tell him you were meeting with teach-ers each day after school to try to catch up. But next week, when they're practicing for the division championship, you need to be there," Alex said.

I held up my left arm as if that was explanation enough. Plus, it was the last two games of the season, the two most important games, and I had absolutely no clue how to even play, never mind offer useful advice as I watched from the bench.

"Not being able to play doesn't mean you're not part of the team, Maddy. You need to be there. You're going to lose your co-captain spot if you're not careful. There's only so much I can do to keep that from happening, and you need that on your college applications if you want to play at that level."

It was the "only so much" that had me worried.

"Jenna wants to be Snow Ball queen. She's after you as well," I said, and Alex shrugged as if that was old news. "Are you sleeping with her?"

"No." His answer was curt and quick, and at least he had the presence of mind to look offended. "We've been through this how many times, Maddy? Why do you keep asking?"

Because I'd overheard her talking in the hall. Because she'd clearly said that she was after Alex. Because I hadn't trusted her since the first day she came to my house freshman year, all makeup and fake smiles.

"She's made no secret about the fact that she wants you," I said.

"Yeah, but she's not the one I love."

He reached out to stroke my cheek, and I pulled away. "I don't believe you anymore."

"Believe what, Maddy? That I am not sleeping with Jenna or that I love you?"

I had no doubt that Alex loved my sister. And I knew for a fact she loved him. But I couldn't shake what Jenna had said in the bathroom—that sympathy points were absolutely working in her favor when it came to Alex.

"You seem pretty friendly with her, more so lately." I didn't know if that was true. For all I knew, Jenna was always fawning over Alex, but right now, for this conversation, I didn't think it mattered. "And I know she's been talking to you a lot about what's going on at home, looking to you to make things better for her."

"She mentioned that you said something to her about her father and money. I asked you not to, Maddy, but you did it anyway."

I had. I was pissed, and she had it coming. I wouldn't apologize; I wasn't sorry. "So you and Jenna—"

Alex shrugged, and my heart sank. "We spent a lot of time together in school when you were out recovering from the accident. You refused to talk to her, made me be the one to answer her calls and relay information. What did you expect?"

I resisted the urge to answer, to yell that his getting close to Jenna was in no way my fault. That I had expected him to give me some time, not run to Jenna for comfort. Instead, I shook my head and ground my nails deeper into my palms.

"I'm not sleeping with her," Alex said.

I didn't know how to respond to that. Just because they hadn't had sex didn't mean something wasn't going on. It didn't make all the time he spent with her okay.

"You're different now, Maddy," he continued. "Distant and quiet. I can't even get you to open up to me, never mind your friends."

I thought about challenging him, asking him what he thought our conversation in the hall yesterday afternoon was about, but I didn't. I went on the defensive: "What does that have to do with anything?"

"Nothing, but it's nice to spend time with somebody who knew the old you."

The old me? The original Maddy? Even Alex, the boy who ignored every indication that I wasn't Maddy, was beginning to doubt me. And without him, I couldn't navigate this lie . . . this life of Maddy's. I'd killed my sister, and then in some attempt to give her back her life, I'd completely destroyed the one good thing she had—Alex.

"If I try harder, if I start talking to you about what happened and going to parties and field hockey practice again, will you stop spending so much time with Jenna? Will you stop letting her come between us?"

He leaned his head back and closed his eyes, then sighed as he shook his head. "I don't know. I don't think you *can* go back to the way you used to be. I don't think anybody could after going through that."

I knew what he was saying—it wasn't Jenna who had driven a wedge between Alex and me, it was me. Alex and my parents were the one constant in this whole mess, and they were starting to slip away.

I could feel the tears building behind my lashes and cursed them. Tears weren't going to help me and they couldn't bring my sister back. And at the end of the day, that was the only thing I wanted—my sister. Alive. The promise that they'd call her name right after mine at graduation. The knowledge that even if we went to separate colleges, she'd only be a phone call or a spring break away. I wanted to meet her future husband for the first time over dinner, and laugh as Dad grilled him with asinine questions. I wanted to help her pick out her wedding dress and complain about the short maid-of-honor dress she'd undoubtedly make me wear. And I wanted *our* kids to play hide-and-seek in Mom and Dad's house while Maddy and I did the dishes and served up dessert. That was what I wanted. That was what I needed, and it wasn't ever going to happen.

Alex reached for my hand, and I let him take it. "It's not that I don't love you, Maddy. God, I so do, but I am beginning to think I'm not the one to help you get past this."

Nobody could help me get past this.

I yanked my hand away and shoved it underneath my legs. I didn't want to be touched, or consoled, or eased into being dumped. At this point, I wanted to be left alone.

I quickly swiped at the lone tear I could feel rolling

down my cheek. Until a month ago, I didn't even like Alex Furey and couldn't figure out why my sister was so utterly fascinated with him. But he'd come to visit me every day in the hospital, stopped by each night while I was at home. He did everything he could think of to try to pull me out of the darkness in my mind. And when I'd come back to school, he protected me, shielded me from the questions and speculation. That was what Maddy saw in him. That was the Alex she knew and loved. And I'd destroyed that like I'd destroyed her.

"Go," I told him. He started to argue with me, and I pushed him away. "I'm fine, Alex, go."

He kissed my cheek before reaching into the backseat for his bag. "I love you, Maddy. That won't ever change."

The cold air hit me as he opened the door, the few pieces of paper I had left on the floor taking flight. Alex caught a gum wrapper, balled it up, and shoved it into his coat pocket. The other piece of paper, the one I'd been carrying around in my back pocket, the one about Molly, managed to make it outside the car. He picked it up and stared at it, his face going white as he realized what it was.

Dropping his bag to the ground, he climbed back into my car and locked the door. Tossing the article onto the dashboard, he turned in his seat to face me. "Talk, Maddy. Now."

38

"Why are you bringing this up?" Alex asked. "You put this behind you a long time ago, Maddy. *We* put it behind us. Leave it there."

Maddy hadn't put it behind her. She'd buried it in a shoe box in her closet with a bag of pills. And judging from the most recent addition to her quasi scrapbook, which incidentally was a copy of the anime club's September newsletter, she had revisited the memory often.

I suspected Maddy's interest in Molly's drug tests was more than friendly concern. It wasn't like Maddy had kept shoe box files on her other friends. But judging from the panic I could see written across Alex's face, I'd have bet my life—if I still had mine to give—that Maddy felt guilty, that she'd done something she regretted and couldn't fix. Something that had been slowly, painfully eating her alive.

Now I needed to figure out how deep that connection went. "Why did you let me do it? If you love me so much, then why didn't you stop me?"

I held my breath as I waited for his response, hoping that I was wrong and Maddy had nothing to do with any of this.

"If you remember correctly, I tried. I told you it wasn't worth it, that I didn't care if you were captain of the field hockey team or a JV player who never made it off the bench," Alex said.

"That's not true," I said, baiting him so he'd tell me more. Alex loved being popular, he and Maddy both did.

"So you're guilty of what—giving her one too many beers last year at one of my parties? Let it go at that, Maddy. For both our sakes, please, let it go at that."

"I didn't just give her a beer," I fired back. I was walking a fine line now and risked exposing myself. But I needed the truth. I needed to know what huge secret of Maddy's I was supposed to live with. "I have the bag of pills."

"Jesus, Maddy. Why didn't you get rid of them? Why are you hanging on to them?" Alex shook his head, his tone softening. "You slipped a pill into her beer on Saturday night. It's not like you had any idea that they were going to test the entire team at Sunday's practice. It's not like you would've done it had you known."

I held my hand up for him to stop. I knew what had

happened to her next. I'd read it five thousand times in Maddy's little collection of facts. Molly had tested positive and got kicked off the team. The colleges that were scouting her were no longer interested, and she found herself in rehab for a drug problem she didn't have. And when she came back, none of her friends wanted anything to do with her.

Maddy wasn't stupid. She had to believe, on some level, that this was completely her fault. And now she was trapped, living with guilt about what had happened. Not unlike me. But she had had Alex to get her through it, to tell her to let it go. I didn't have anybody anymore. Not even Josh.

"I don't understand why I did it in the first place, why I cared. She was our friend, Alex. Why would I want to screw over my friend like that?"

He looked at me as if I were crazy. "It was the beginning of our junior year, Maddy. We were finally upperclassmen. You were elected homecoming queen, and I had been given a starting position on the soccer team. You . . . we had everything you ever wanted, except—"

"Except what? Being co-captain of the field hockey team?" It seemed like such a selfish reason. My emotions shifted. I didn't feel bad for Maddy anymore. I was angry, disgusted that my sister had been so catty and concerned with her own popularity that she would treat someone like that.

"Yeah. That is exactly what you wanted, what I as-

258

sumed you still wanted. Jenna was a shoo-in; it was be-tween you and Molly. You know how it goes, captain spots go to the team members who clock the most play-ing time, the best players. You and Molly . . . you were both goalies. If she had missed Sunday practice or played crappy because she was sick, the second captain spot would have gone to you. You weren't trying to ruin her life, Maddy, just eliminate her chances of becoming co-captain."

"Of course Jenna was a shoo-in." The mere mention of Jenna's name had my blood boiling. The more I learned about Maddy's life, about her friends, the less I liked Jenna. She had her hands in everything, and none of it was good.

"Don't blame this on her, Maddy. She may have given you the idea, but you are the one who actually did it."

"Wait. What?"

"You and I talked about this for days. I told you to let it go. It didn't matter to me whether you were captain or not. I doubt it mattered to your parents or the colleges you wanted to apply to. You were good, that was enough."

"Molly was good, too," I mumbled, remembering the one game of my sister's I went to. Molly played that day, and she was as good as, if not better than, Maddy.

"She was. But remember, it wasn't about Molly. It was about Jenna. You were the one who didn't want to be one-upped by Jenna."

I already knew the answer to the question I was about

to ask. Jenna had made it pretty clear earlier today, but I asked anyway, wanting to see exactly whose side Alex was on. "So she knows. This whole time she's known that I drugged Molly and she hasn't said a word? Hasn't tried to use it against me? Don't you find that the least bit odd?"

Alex flinched, as if what I said had caught him off guard. "Of course she knows. Her older brother got the pills for you. And no, she would never use it against you. She can be conniving sometimes, I'll give you that, but she is not that cold."

I thought about selling her out to Alex, clueing him in to her little ultimatum in the bathroom. It took me less than a second to decide not to. That'd make me no better than Jenna.

But I wasn't going to let that comment go unanswered either. "I don't think you know Jenna as well as you think you do, Alex."

"Maybe it's you I don't know as well as I used to."

He was spot-on there. "Probably."

Neither of us said anything after that. I'd gotten what I'd come for. I had the answers I had been seeking, but somehow that knowledge didn't help. Having to carry the weight of my sister's secret was something I wasn't prepared to do. I hadn't signed on for this. I could play Barbie doll, pretend I wasn't smart, and fake interest in things I hated, but this . . . I didn't know what to do with this.

Sitting here in the dark with Alex waiting for the rest of my world to crumble down wasn't going to help either. "I don't know what to say." I didn't look at him when I spoke, didn't have the energy to dissect the emotions playing across his face.

"I don't think there is anything else to say."

Alex tore the newspaper clipping in two and shoved it in his coat pocket. He could destroy that one and the dozen others sitting in that shoe box if he wanted to. It wouldn't change anything.

He opened the car door and got out. "Go home, Maddy, and forget about this. It wasn't your fault, and there is nothing you can do to change what happened."

I disagreed. An apology to Molly would be a good start.

"Take tomorrow off from school and get a handle on yourself. I'll cover for you, tell everybody you have a doctor's appointment or something. I'll pick you up at three and take you to your field hockey game. And on Monday . . ."

Alex didn't finish his thought, but I didn't need him to. I knew what he meant. On Monday, I had to get up and do it over again. Pretend to be my sister, try to find a way to deal with the emptiness that filled me while making point-less conversation with her friends . . . with Jenna.

I waited until Alex had pulled out of the lot to start my car. Going home wasn't an option. Mom was there and Dad was probably trying to coax her out of their room, away from the collection of my stuff she had surrounded herself with. I didn't need another reminder of how I'd messed everything up.

I pulled out my phone and texted the one lie I was sure Dad would buy: *Staying at Jenna's.*

It took a few minutes, but the phone finally chimed with a simple message: *Have fun.*

I drove around for hours that night, pulled into our driveway twice, then pulled back out. I would've gone to talk to Maddy, curled up on the ground beneath my own name, but the cemetery gates were locked at dusk, leaving me with nowhere to go.

It was past midnight when I pulled up across the street from Josh's house. The house was dark, the streetlight at the end of his driveway broken and flickering to its death. That's where I spent the night—in my car, parked across the street from Josh's, watching, remembering, and dreaming about what I would've done differently had I known, as soon as I woke up in the hospital, that he loved me, too.

39

The sharp rap on the window jarred me awake. I snapped my head up, making contact with the back of my seat. My neck hurt, not from the sudden motion but from sleeping hunched over my steering wheel for the past few hours.

The knock was softer now but equally urgent. I cleared my eyes and looked toward the window. The thin layer of ice covering the glass made it difficult to see, but eventually I could make out a face. It was Josh. He had his hat and gloves on, his backpack slung over one shoulder. I turned on the car and jacked up the heat before rolling down the window.

"What are you doing here?" he asked.

I looked past him to his driveway. Kim was standing there staring straight at me.

"I asked you what you are doing here," Josh said again.

"Nothing."

"Go home, *Maddy*."

"But—" I started to argue, to tell him to stop calling me that, to give me a second chance, but he waved me off.

"You had your chance yesterday. There's nothing here for you anymore."

I didn't wait for him to walk away this time, couldn't stomach watching him get in the car with Kim. I put my car in gear and left, driving until I hit the town line. I sat there for hours, parked in the breakdown lane with my flashers on, literally feet away from a new town . . . a new life.

Nobody stopped to help me. Not one cop or Good Samaritan pulled over to see if I needed help. Funny how I could sit here for two hours and seventeen minutes and not one of the hundreds of people who drove by thought to stop. Yet spend two seconds acting weird in the high school cafeteria and you were suddenly the object of everybody's attention.

A thousand thoughts flew through my mind about Molly and what my sister had unintentionally set into motion. I knew Maddy was sorry for what she'd done. I could feel it in my heart, saw it in the tears she'd tried to hide the night of Alex's party. And I'd taken away her chance to apologize to Molly.

The emptiness I'd been struggling to overcome settled around me like a dark, unwavering cloud. My sister, my best friend, the one who shared my birthday, was gone.

Forever. And it was there on the side of the road, as I raged in my car, screamed and cried and cursed my sister for leaving me, that I finally embraced the pain and made my decision.

I turned the car around in the middle of the road and drove, without thinking, back to school, back to the two people I wanted to apologize to first.

The school parking lot was full. I could either wedge my car between the Dumpster and the buses-only zone in front of the school or park way over on the other side of the fields. The Dumpster-buses-only spot worked; I wasn't planning on being here long anyway.

I didn't bother to sign myself in. The front office had probably already marked me absent. By the time the school secretary got around to calling my parents this afternoon, it'd be too late. By then, they would know the truth.

It was noon, and the hallways were crowded with kids at their lockers swapping out books for their next class or going to lunch. The fact that I was wearing the same clothes as yesterday didn't go unnoticed. I could see people pointing as clearly as I heard their hushed comments. My hair was pulled into a messy ponytail, and what little was left of yesterday's makeup was smudged. I didn't care. I was done pretending. I was done trying to fit in. I was . . . done.

The cafeteria doors were closed, the roar of noise inside barely audible from the hall. But I knew they were there.

It went dead silent the minute I walked in, one hundred and twenty-nine senior heads and a handful of under-classmen turning in my direction. I didn't have to waste time trying to find them, they'd be in their assigned sections of hell. Molly was at the end of Maddy's table, a safe three empty chairs between her and everybody else. Alex was sitting there, too, Maddy's friends crowded around him and Jenna cozying up to his side.

Alex pushed Jenna away when I walked in, the color draining from his face. Dismay—no, fear was what I saw in his expression, pure fear. "Maddy," he called out, his eyes signaling me over.

I shook my head and walked toward Molly. I'd get to Alex, but not yet. Molly had been kind to me, extending her friendship and an offer to help. Because of that, she was going to be first.

Alex was up and out of his seat the minute he realized I wasn't going to quietly retreat to the hall and wait for him. "This isn't what I call laying low," he said.

I actually laughed at his words, a distorted chuckle that took even me by surprise. "I'm not trying to lay low, Alex." *I'm trying to fix what I did,* I finished silently to myself. "I'm sorry I took Maddy from you, sorry I can't be the girl you used to know, you used to love."

"Let me take you home. We can talk about this there."

"No, I don't want to talk about it." *Not anymore.*

"Nobody expects you to be the same Maddy."

"I expected it, Alex. I tried, I really did. For you, for my parents, for everyone, I tried." I took out the original drawing I'd made of Maddy three years ago and handed it to him. I'd looked for a half hour the other day before I finally found it underneath a pile of old Barbie dolls in my closet. "It's not very good, but it's yours."

His eyes scanned mine for some sort of explanation. I swallowed hard and counted to three, then told him the truth. "I can't be her anymore. It hurts too much to be her. I don't want to spend my days trying to dress and act and talk like my sister. I want to spend them remembering her illogical hatred of my dog and her love of lavender-scented shampoo. I want to cry for her, miss her, and I want everyone to know just how much Maddy being gone hurts, does that make sense?"

He shook his head, the shocking knowledge of what I was saying finally settling in as he whispered my name. *"Ella?"*

I nodded and took a quick look at Jenna. She had her hand on Alex's arm as if somehow it was *her* support he needed. "She's right. You deserve better than I can give you."

Jenna's grin widened at my comment and she moved in closer to Alex, as if telling me who owned him now.

"I know you think Jenna is what you want. What you need," I continued. "But she's not. Trust me, she'll take everything good in you and destroy it and Maddy wouldn't want that."

"How dare you—" Jenna began to argue, no doubt to tell me how pathetic and wrong I was.

I cut her off. "You, I have nothing to say to. You're cold and calculating and not worth my time."

I walked away, relieved that I was almost done. Molly sat there watching me, her smile genuine. "Feels good, doesn't it?" she said.

I nodded. It felt great to finally tell the truth, to lay into Jenna after years of listening to her belittle me. "But it is you I owe the biggest apology to."

"No you don't. I get why you kept your distance." Molly kicked the chair out across from her and motioned for me to sit down. "But none of that matters now."

I slid the chair back in and watched as the hope slowly drained from her face. She had thought I was going to sit down and be her friend, forget about the other end of the table and stick with her. I would've had I not already made up my mind.

"There is a seat at that table if ever you want it," I said as I pointed to the table Josh and I always sat at. "I know it won't make up for what happened to you last year, but I thought perhaps some *real* friends and an apology would be a start."

She looked confused. "I don't understand," Molly said.

"I didn't either until last night. You were up for the co-captain spot on the field hockey team. You were good, probably better than Maddy. The other spot was going to—"

"Jenna," she said, finishing my sentence.

"If you were hungover or sick, then you'd miss the

268

mandatory Sunday practice and probably lose your chance of being co-captain. At the very least, you'd play like crap for the first quarter and then Coach would have no choice but to pull you out."

Her eyes darted between me and Jenna, and I swear I saw a flash of understanding in her eyes. "What are you trying to say?"

"Maddy slipped something into your drink that Saturday night. She was trying to make you sick, figured you wouldn't be able to make practice the next day. I don't think she ever imagined they'd test the team, I can't believe my sister—"

She was staring at me as if I were a stranger, as if the words pouring out of my mouth were somehow not mine.

"I'm sorry," I said. "I know that doesn't even begin to make up for what happened to you, but I don't know what else to say. Don't know how to make it right."

Molly shook her head, a look of complete disbelief clouding her expression. "I don't get it. You, I mean Maddy, talked to me at the party before she left, told me she'd pick me up early the next day so we could go check out Lincoln High's sweeper, that she was one of the best in the state and if we could figure out her weakness, then we'd have the upper hand."

"She still is," I said. I knew exactly what girl Molly was referring to. Maddy had idolized her, talked about her constantly during field hockey season, how she wished she had half that girl's skills. "Except now she plays for Boston College, not Lincoln High."

Somehow what I was saying finally clicked and she stood up, her chair falling to the floor behind her as she leaned across the table so her face was mere inches from mine. "Who else knew?" Her voice came out in a shudder, like the words were stuck there and had to be shaken free. "Who else knew that she drugged me?"

I saw Alex make a move toward me, Jenna dropping into the chair behind him. Alex had nothing to be afraid of. He'd had no part in this. In fact, he'd tried to talk my sister out of it for days. And as for Jenna, she still wasn't worth the effort.

"Nobody," I said, and I swear I heard a collective sigh of relief. "No one else knew. But I'm sorry. My sister was, too, and I wanted you to know that."

Molly fell forward onto the table, her hands bracing herself at either side of her head as she fought to fully understand the weight of what I'd unloaded on her.

"Here," I said as I dropped the letter to the table. I'd written it last night in front of Josh's house. It explained what my sister had done to Molly and why. I went so far as to say it was Maddy and Maddy alone who had concocted the crazy plan. Not for Jenna's sake—God knows I didn't care about her—but for Alex's. Jenna would surely try to implicate him. I didn't want to destroy his chances at playing college soccer like Maddy had destroyed Molly's chances of playing college field hockey.

I'd signed my sister's name to the confession, then dated it the day before the accident. I understood the pain and guilt Maddy had been carrying around, her desire to tell the truth, and the fear that came along with that. This was my way of giving her the forgiveness and the sense of peace I was still struggling to find, of letting her apologize to Molly the way I knew she'd wanted to . . . like she had planned to. Plus, I hoped Molly could use it to get into college, maybe explain to the scouts why they needed to take a second look at her.

"I don't know if it will help, but it's spelled out there for everybody to see. What Maddy did to you was unforgivable, and I think she knew that. I think that was what she was trying to tell you that night at the party." *The last night any of us saw her alive,* I silently added. "But I am sorry for lying to you, for lying to everybody."

I turned and walked through the doors, intent on making it out of the cafeteria and out of the school before I lost the courage to come clean to my parents.

I wasn't more than a few steps out the door when the cafeteria erupted into chaos, everybody talking and reaching for their phones. In less than a few seconds, everything I had said would be broadcast to the world, uploaded and texted to everybody . . . including my parents.

40

There was a note tacked to the refrigerator. The handwriting was small and shaky, but I recognized it as Mom's. She'd gone to the office with Dad. He had a few hours of work to catch up on before they had an appointment with a grief counselor. The address was written below the counselor's name on the off chance that I wanted to join them. I wasn't going. No counselor, no amount of framed diplomas on an office wall could get me out of the hole I'd dug. After that, they were going to get dinner. She said she'd call and let me know where they were going in case Alex and I wanted to join them after the game. I didn't.

I looked at the clock on the microwave—it was 1:00. I'd never been to a shrink before, but I presumed my parents would be there awhile. They had a lot of stuff to hash out, stuff that was mainly my fault. My guess was they'd last about an hour, maybe more if Mom cried. That gave me a couple of hours, at least, before I had to face them.

I grabbed my phone and shut it off, going so far as to remove the battery from the back and shove the phone into the top drawer of my desk. I didn't want to talk to anybody, at least not until I figured out exactly what I was going to say to my parents.

I went into my own closet and pulled out my favorite pair of jeans, the ones that Josh and I used to draw on when we were bored in History class. Each character, each symbol, and each silly quote had a story attached to it. I wanted to wrap myself in those memories and carry them with me. The flannel shirt was one of Maddy's. It was soft and well worn, something she used to wear on the weekends when she was lounging around. It had a lipstick smudge on the sleeve and still smelled like her—lavender and vanilla, and the tiniest hint of Alex's cologne that always seemed to linger around her. The sweatshirt Josh gave me the other day was still hanging on the chair downstairs. I grabbed it and put it on, drawing an overly long sleeve to my nose and breathing in the familiar inky scent that was Josh.

It felt good to surround myself with the warm scents of the two people I loved most, and without having to worry about my hair or makeup, I felt like regular old me. The only things missing were my sneakers and my sketchbook. I'd grab those in a minute.

"Hey, Bailey," I said as I ruffled his fur. "You recognized me from the start. Nobody else did but you."

He nuzzled my hand and rolled over, looking for me to scratch his belly. I reached for the box of treats Mom hadn't moved from my nightstand. I hid the entire box underneath the comforter. If he could get at it, then they were his, my gift for making him suffer this past month without me. "I'll see you in a little bit, buddy. You stay here and find your treats."

I left him there pawing through my bed and went back into Maddy's room to grab my wallet. I stopped midstep when I saw a dress wrapped in clear plastic lying on the bed. There was an alteration slip attached with a pick-up date of today. No wonder I couldn't find the dress Maddy had bought for the Snow Ball. She'd taken it to be fitted the week before she died.

It was short and black, and there was a brand-new pair of heels sitting next to it. On top of the dress was a note from Mom instructing me to try it on in case it needed to be re-altered. I knew what she was getting at. I was thinner than before the accident, had been eating less.

I put down the note and picked up the silver box next to the dress. Inside was a pair of diamond earrings and a matching pendant. I recognized them. Grammy had given them to my mom before she died.

Maddy's shoe box collection of memories was still in the closet, where I'd left it, the ones about Molly still tucked beneath the mattress. I reached to get them and pulled out every reference to Molly. I tore them into a million pieces and tossed them in the trash, then flushed the pills down the toilet. I never wanted Mom and Dad to find out what Maddy had done, never wanted their image of her tainted in any way. But that wasn't in my hands anymore. That was up to Molly, and no matter what she decided to do with the information I'd handed her, I'd stand beside her, be the kind of friend she deserved.

I walked into my parents' room to leave them a note. Last time I was there, Mom had my drawings scattered across her floor. They were still there, but now stacked neatly on Dad's nightstand. I sifted through them until I found my favorite. It was a drawing of the tire swing that hung in Josh's backyard. The rope was tattered, the tire barely there, but I loved that swing.

I turned the sketch over, my hands hovering over the blank page, unsure of what to write. A plain *I'm sorry* seemed too simplistic; the truth too complicated. What I finally settled on was this:

I'm Ella

I left the note on my parents' bed, where I knew Mom would find it. She'd have questions for me when I got home, ones I had no idea how to answer. But I would, I would tell them everything and then pray they'd find a way to forgive me.

There was no going back. I knew telling my parents

I wasn't Maddy would destroy them. Mom needed Maddy, not Ella . . . not the quiet, independent Ella who always shut them out. But I couldn't do it anymore, couldn't get up every morning and fight to be someone I wasn't, someone I'd never wanted to be.

And Josh, well, I was pretty sure I'd messed that up. But at the end of the day, he had Kim. She was simple and loyal and tried so hard to please him. She could make him happy in a way I never could.

41

It was always cold and damp. No matter what day I came or what the sky looked like when I left the house, it always seemed to be cold and wet here. Maybe it was an omen. More likely just typical November weather in Rhode Island.

The granite marker bearing my name glistened in the rain, like tiny jewels reflecting a light that wasn't there. It reminded me of Maddy, of the bangles and sparkly accessories she always wore. Even in death, buried six feet below a tombstone engraved with the wrong name, she found a way to shine through, making this morbid place her own.

I closed my eyes and counted to five before speaking the words I'd been holding back for so long. "I'm Ella. I'm not you. I never could be you. I never wanted to be you. I tried . . . for you, I tried, but I can't do it anymore."

Relief and pain fought for control, those simple words a torturous reminder of what I'd done. Sighing, I closed my eyes and surrendered to the truth. That was what I wanted. That was what I'd been struggling to say since the second I realized I wasn't my sister and never could be.

"I. Am. Ella. Lawton." I said it again, reveling in the sound of my own name, the sense of complete peace it brought.

A warm hand grazed my shoulder, and I gasped. I'd thought I was alone, thought I had more time to practice my confession before I actually came clean to the rest of the world.

"Hey, Ella," she said. "It's nice to meet you, officially that is."

Molly held out her hand and I took it, not sure what else I was supposed to do. "I was telling the truth in the cafeteria. I'm really *not* Maddy," I said, confused as to why she wasn't angry with me, wasn't calling me demented and insane for impersonating my dead sister.

"I know. The entire school knows. You pretty much told them all in the cafeteria today."

"Why are you here? How did you know I was here?" I had expected Josh to come looking for me. He wasn't in the cafeteria when I apologized to Molly and Alex, but I figured it wouldn't have taken long for the news to reach him. I even secretly wished my parents would come find me once they got home and saw my note. But I never imagined it'd be Molly, the girl whose life my sister had nearly destroyed.

"I wasn't done talking to you in the cafeteria. You weren't at home, so I asked Josh where he thought you'd go, and he told me here, so . . ." Molly held her arms out wide as if that was explanation enough. It wasn't.

"Josh, I get," I said. He was my best friend, of course he would know where to find me. He'd been figuring me out for years, knew me better than I knew myself most days. "But why do you care?"

Molly dropped to the ground next to me, not caring that her white jeans were now covered in mud. "You can't trade one life for another. Trust me, Ella. Maddy's life . . . you don't want it."

I knew that. With every fiber of my being I knew that I could never be Maddy.

"So why aren't you mad now?" I had braced myself for everybody's anger, for them to be pissed beyond belief at what I'd done. This . . . this quiet understanding, I didn't know what to do with it. "I lied to you. To everybody. Why aren't you angry?"

Molly shrugged. "I don't know. I guess I liked watching Alex stumble around you, and I kinda liked you, Ella. That, and it was nice to finally have a friend again."

"You think everybody will hate me? You think my parents will? I mean, I know Josh does."

"Josh? Hate you? Never. He'll forgive you. He can't

279

help himself. That kid has had a thing for you since the first day your sister pawned you off on him. Everybody could see that."

Everybody but me, that is. "What about—"

"Your parents?" she interrupted, and I nodded. "No. I mean, they'll probably be confused more than anything. They'll blame themselves for a while. I know my parents did. But eventually, you will sort it out."

Molly understood what I was going through. She knew how hard it was to rebuild a life from a past that you wanted to forget, a past that you had absolutely no control over. "I don't know what I am going to do."

"I do." Her voice was filled with a confidence I'd never heard from her before, and I prayed that a small sliver of her strength would find its way into me. "You're going to get up off this wet ground, leave your sister's life behind, and start living yours. I'm not gonna lie; it's going to suck for a while. People are going to look at you differently, call you messed up and selfish. God knows Jenna will probably accuse you of being jealous, of pretending to be Maddy so that you could get Alex and be popular. But I'll be there to help you."

She paused and looked back toward the road. "And he'll be there to help you, too."

I followed her gaze and saw Josh standing there. I knew he'd heard everything I'd said, from the confession to the justifications I laid on Molly, the same ones I used on him.

"Has he been there the whole time?" I asked.

"Yep," Molly said. "Did you think he would actually have let me come alone? Not a chance. As I said, that boy can't help himself when it comes to you."

Molly got up and brushed what she could of the mud from her pants, then took a step back. "If you ask me, I think Alex always knew you weren't Maddy. He just didn't care. That's why he fought so hard to make everything seem perfect between the two of you and to cover for you."

I knew what she was trying to say. He wanted Maddy, wanted *me* to be Maddy so much that he ignored the truth, hid from it like I had.

With one last encouraging nod, Molly turned and walked away. She stopped when she reached her car and called back, "You know what happened with your sister and the drugs? Well, that is done and over with. As far as I am concerned, that incident was buried with Maddy."

"Thanks," I said. I'd already done enough damage to Maddy's name. I didn't want her to suffer anymore.

42

My eyes scanned the nearly empty cemetery.
When I woke up in the hospital, when everybody, including myself, thought I was Maddy, there were dozens of people there waiting for me to open my eyes. Here, on the day I was bringing Ella back, there were only Molly and Josh. But somehow that was okay. The person who mattered to me most was standing a few gravestones away, waiting for me to make the first move.

Josh held out his hand, softly beckoning me forward. He was the last person I wanted to hurt and the one person I didn't think of when I made my choice to live a lie. When I didn't move, he came to me.

"Hey, Ella."

"I'm sorry." It seemed completely inadequate, but I said it anyway. I was sorry for what my sister did to Molly. Sorry for taking my sister's life in every way possible. Sorry for lying to my parents. And sorry for not trusting Josh with the truth from the beginning.

I slipped my hand into his and let his warmth comfort me. I didn't know which one of us needed the physical contact more, but it made no difference either way. We both needed the reassurance that this was real, that I was finally admitting who I was and reclaiming my own life.

I turned and looked up into his eyes, silently thanking him for being here and never giving up on me. His eyes weren't red-rimmed like mine, but they were glossy, letting me know he'd also been crying.

I ran my hand across his cheek. It was soft and strong like him. He stared at me, his eyes distant and sad as if unsure, or maybe too scared, to believe I was finally me. I couldn't blame him. For so long I wasn't.

I'd never touched him like this before—gently, intimately, like he meant more to me than anything else in this world. He did; and if he'd listen to me, give me a second chance to explain, I'd tell him.

"I love you, too," I whispered. "Since the day Maddy introduced me to you, it's been you."

Josh's eyes brightened at my words and he squeezed my hand tighter.

His silence troubled me. "It's me. Ella. I mean, I'm not going to pretend to be Maddy anymore. Not with you, not with my parents, not with anybody," I promised.

Josh looked down at the gravestone bearing my name. His hand shook in mine, and I was too afraid to break the forgiving quiet with words. I mumbled another apology and looked away.

"I was pissed at you, Ella, angry that you lied and hurt that you wouldn't trust me with the truth, but that never changed the way I felt about you. I'm sorry that I wasn't there in the hospital when you woke up, sorry that I didn't stay with Alex and see for myself who you were."

"What I did . . . why I did it had nothing to do with you. You don't need to apologize. You didn't do anything wrong."

"I did everything wrong," Josh said. "I should've told you I loved you the minute I realized it. I should've continued to tell you every day I saw you. I should've made you go to your parents and tell them you weren't Maddy the minute I figured it out. *I* should've told them myself. I should have—"

I held a finger up to his lips, silencing him. "And I shouldn't have lied."

The tears he'd been holding in finally fell, his eyes glinting with hope and promise. Everybody I needed was right there, including Maddy. As long as I had Josh, then somehow, everything—the accident, Maddy's death, me pretending to be somebody I wasn't—was going to be okay.

"I have something for you." Josh pulled his hand away from mine and dug into his front pocket. His fingers curled around the object he'd yanked out. Whatever it was, it was tiny, completely eclipsed by his fingers.

"What is it?" I asked. When he opened his hand, a

thin multicolored string fell between his fingers. I took it, turning the string bracelet over and over. I could see where the doctors had cut it off in the ER, where Josh had tried to piece it back together.

"Where did you get this?" I asked.

"I looked for it when I got to the hospital, to see which one of you had it on, but they'd cut it off. There was a pile of your stuff in the hall . . . both your things. I went through it and took it."

"Why?"

Josh shrugged. "I wanted it."

I handed it back to him and held out my wrist. "No, give me your foot," he said as he knelt down in the wet grass. I felt his hands on my ankle. They were shaking like mine. "I did the best I could to fix the strings they cut in the ER," he said as he tied off the last knot. "I know it's not perfect, and I'll buy matching ones for our wrists tomorrow, but I want you to wear it anyway."

The tears I'd seen moments earlier were gone, his eyes now full of nervous anticipation. "I've missed you," he said, and stood up, his hands toying with the damp strands of hair falling around my face. He was so close, close enough that I could see the flecks of gray in his green eyes.

"I have waited forever to do this, Ella, and I nearly lost you twice in the process."

I suppose I should've waited for him, let Josh close those final two inches between us. But my stomach twisted in anticipation, my mind close to freezing up. I had waited for that moment for so long, had dreamed about it.

Ignoring my fear, I reached up and ran my hands through his hair, tugging gently until he got my hint. I didn't want to wait anymore. I didn't want to lose another second to fear or uncertainty.

He stopped as his lips met mine, his words whispered across my breath. "I love you, Ella Lawton. If you believe in nothing else, I need you to believe in that."

I shook my head as he tried to swipe at my tears with his nose. I wanted to cry. I needed to cry. For the past, for the future, for him.

"And I love you, too." Those words were an extension of me, every syllable of their meaning saving me from myself.

I heard rather than saw the car come to a stop, the tires screeching to a halt as the car door opened. They didn't bother to turn the engine off or shut their doors. They got out and ran those few short steps to where I stood.

Josh grabbed my hand, probably afraid that I'd bolt. I wouldn't. They already knew; the simple note I'd left them was still in my mom's hand.

They looked so different, sad and hopeful at the same time. Mom smiled, the first true display of happiness I'd seen from her in weeks, and it was for me. Dad mouthed my name, my real name, then nodded. They knew who I was, what I'd done, and they'd come to find me anyway.

"Hi." It seemed like such a silly way to start the conversation, but it was the only thing I could think of, the one word that solidified in the jumbled mess of emotions pouring out of me.

"This is Ella. Ella, these are your parents," Josh said, and I laughed at the insanely sweet way he tried to smooth out the tense silence that surrounded us.

Dad chuckled, too, then held out his hand in a mock gesture of greeting. "Nice to have you back. I'm your father and this lovely lady standing next to me is your mom."

I took his hand, fully aware he was going to pull me into his arms. I let him, burying myself in his chest and holding on like he was the last solid thing left in the world.

"We've missed you."

The whispered words came from behind me, and I lifted my head enough to see Mom staring at me before she kissed the top of my head. I wiggled free, confused as to why they weren't upset with me. I'd expected anger . . . for the accident, for lying, for taking what good memories they had of Maddy and destroying them. I was prepared for that, was prepared to accept that. But this, this silent forgiveness . . . I didn't know what to do with it.

"You're not angry," I said as my head whipped between Mom and Dad. I was waiting, wondering which one of them was going to lose it on me first. Neither did. Mom shook her head, and Dad held out his arms again, offering me shelter and comfort.

"Why? I don't get it, why aren't you mad?"

"We're sorry that you thought you had to do this. Sorry that you ever thought Maddy was more important to us than you. We are confused and angry with ourselves for not recognizing who you were the instant you woke up, but we're not upset with you, Ella. We couldn't be."

Ella. The sound of my name coming from my mother had me shaking, seeking out my father's hand as the weight of the lie I'd been carrying finally lifted. I sucked in a ragged breath and then another one after that, my heart, my soul, my entire being realigning itself with the truth that everybody now knew: I was Ella Lawton.

I reached out a hand to Josh, pulled him into the circle my parents' arms had created around me. Somehow I knew it was going to be okay. Everything I needed was here, enveloping me. And as for Maddy, she was my sister, my first and best friend. Here or not, she was part of me and I would carry her with me forever.

Like Molly said, it wasn't going to be easy—there would be gossip, and questions, and a crapload of family therapy—but I'd take it, because right there, standing at the grave of my sister, my life literally started over.

EPILOGUE

I had a few more boxes to unpack, most of them extra toiletries Mom insisted I needed. The room was smaller than I'd expected—nothing more than a shoe box with two identical beds, two desks, and two closets. I'd managed to jam as much as I could into the small space, even sent a duffle bag of clothes home with my parents, but it still felt overstuffed. Where Mom expected me to hide a year's worth of tampons, I had no idea. I shoved them under the bed with the seven thousand bars of soap and tubes of toothpaste she'd made me keep.

I'd do anything she asked—keep a lifetime's worth of toiletries shoved under my bed and call her every night if that's what she wanted—in the hopes of making up for what I'd done.

According to Mom, this was my chance to start over, to reinvent myself, in a world where nobody knew about my past. But I wouldn't be alone. Instead of the single room I'd wanted, I had a roommate. She wasn't there yet. Her name was Sadie Rose, and she was from Austin, Texas, or so the meet-your-roommate e-mail I'd received in July had said. The message even included a picture of her, not that you could tell much from it. From what I could see, she was blond and apparently had an affinity for thick black eyeliner.

We had exchanged a couple of e-mails, mostly revolving around who was bringing the mini-fridge and who was bringing the microwave. She seemed nice enough.

She had texted me this morning. Her flight had been canceled and she doubted she'd be here before tomorrow afternoon. That was fine by me. It gave me one more day to figure out what to say to her in person.

I left her side of the room completely untouched, taking over what I calculated to be my half of the ten-by-twelve-foot space. I hoped she wouldn't mind which side I'd picked and didn't have space issues; that would suck.

The door to my room opened, and I didn't bother to turn around to see who it was. I already knew. He'd been in and out of my room five times in the last half hour, trying to figure out how to make the wooden bulletin board I brought from home stick to the cinder-block walls.

"The guy at the hardware store said this should work," Josh told me as he held up some double-sided tape. "Although I still don't get why you didn't do what your dad suggested and lean it against the window."

I shrugged. "I like it this way better."

Mom gave both Maddy and me bulletin boards when we started high school. She said it was the perfect way to show off what was important to us without marring our walls. We'd killed our walls anyway, taping pictures to them and nailing up photos, but that didn't stop us from using our bulletin boards to tack up whatever memento was important to us that day.

I'd combined the items from our two boards before I left, took an old concert-ticket stub and the picture of her field hockey team off Maddy's and added it to mine. There was a picture of Molly and me that was taken the day before she left for UNC, the crumpled-up drawing of the tree that had given me away to Josh, and our prom picture—not the formal one but a candid his mom snapped as we were getting into his car. In the center of it all were Maddy's car keys, the ones to the blue Honda that nearly claimed both our lives, and the appointment card for the counselor Mom had found me here. I didn't want to tape these things to random spots on the wall. I wanted them like this— smushed together in one contained, controllable spot. It was a combination of the two of us and I now used it to remind me how strangely similar and oddly different Maddy and I truly were.

"Okay," Josh said as he dropped the tape onto my desk. "If it is that important to you, then I will find a way to make it stick, even if it means holding it up there myself all year."

I laughed. The idea of Josh stuck in my room—in my life—for the next four years was not something I minded. Not in the least.

"What's so funny?" he asked.

"Nothing. You."

"Great," he said as he launched himself onto my bed and held out his arms. His eyes darted to the bare frame and empty mattress across the room, and I knew exactly what he was thinking before he spoke. "What are the chances of your roommate showing up anytime soon?"

"Not good," I said as I snuggled into him. "She texted me this morning. Her flight got canceled, so she won't be here until sometime tomorrow."

"Perfect," Josh said as he pulled me tighter in to his chest. "My roommate's parents are still here, so my room is off-limits for a while."

I'd met his roommate when I was walking Mom and Dad out to their car. They wanted to stop by Josh's room before they left and say goodbye to him. They made Josh promise for the gazillionth time to take care of me and to call them if I seemed distant or depressed. I hadn't been off since the day I finally admitted to the world who I was, since the day I reclaimed my life and let myself mourn my sister. But that didn't stop Mom and Dad from worrying, from being overprotective.

"What's he like?" I asked.

"Who, Todd?" Josh asked as he scooched up on the bed and rolled his eyes. "Let's see. Didn't matter that I was

here first and had my stuff put away, I had to pack everything up and move it to the other side of the room because,
apparently, he absolutely has to have the right side. Everything . . . his binders, his closets, even his sheets are color
coordinated. He made my mother take the TV and DVD
player I brought home because he said it was a distraction,
and if I needed that kind of noise in my life, then there
was no reason I couldn't get it in the common area."

I couldn't help it—I cracked up because seeing Josh
frustrated was funny.

"Oh, it gets better," he said, dead serious, and I did my
best to control my amusement, to stop smiling and look
completely enthralled by his rant.

I couldn't imagine what he was going to come out with
next, but I waved him on, happy that he—that we—were
finally here, talking about normal stuff like roommates
and bulletin boards as opposed to dead sisters and lies.
"How much better?"

"Todd has what I would call an unhealthy fascination
with the Impressionist period. My room is now covered
with pastel prints."

My giggling erupted into a full-blown howl at that. Josh
tried for angry, went so far as to poke me in an attempt to
get me to stop, but even he couldn't stop himself from
seeing the humor in it.

"What about your comic-book and manga drawings? I
take it he doesn't appreciate your talent."

"Appreciate it? According to him, comic books are

for prepubescent boys with bad parental role models and a superhero complex. Yeah . . . we are going to get along fantastically."

"Umm, I bet you are," I said. I gave them two months tops before one of them snapped and demanded a new roommate. My guess was it'd be Josh. Until then, I figured Josh could spend his time here, lounging on my bed studying and drawing.

I picked up the can of soda that was sitting on the windowsill and raised it in a toast. "Here's to hoping my roommate likes you, because from the sounds of it you are practically going to be living here."

Josh took the soda from my hand and deposited it back on the windowsill behind us. I knew what he was doing. I'd seen that look a hundred times before—the sparkle of humor hidden behind intent. His lips were inches from mine, his hands at my hips as he breathed, "That's the plan, Ella. Being here, with you, that was always the plan."

ACKNOWLEDGMENTS

This book does not belong to me, but rather to the people whose patience and faith made it possible. Remembering that: Thanks to my agent, Kevan Lyon, who believed in me even when I didn't believe in myself. To my amazing editor, Janine O'Malley, whose extraordinary vision for this book taught me to dig deeper and write harder than I thought possible. Thanks to my family—Brian, Caroline, Kyle, and Casey—who ate more than their share of takeout as I wrote and edited this book into final form. To my sister, Julie Nelson . . . my first and best friend; my brother, Bill Burgess, for showing me nothing is impossible; and my parents for instilling in me a love of the written word. To the countless CPs whose long-distance moral support kept me going, and my dear friend Cyndie Furey, for having the courage to read everything I have ever written from day one.